Send 'Em South

Young Heroes of History

D0088432

by
Alan N. Kay

WHITE MANE KIDS

This White Mane Books publication
was printed by
Beidel Printing House, Inc.
63 West Burd Street
Shippensburg, PA 17257-0152 USA

In respect for the scholarship contained herein, the acid-free paper used in this book meets the guidelines for permanence and durability of the Committee on Production Guidelines for Book Longevity of the Council on Library Resources.

For a complete list of available publications
please write
White Mane Books
Division of White Mane Publishing Company, Inc.
P.O. Box 152
Shippensburg, PA 17257-0152 USA

Library of Congress Cataloging-in-Publication Data

Kay, Alan N., 1965-
    Send 'em South : young heroes of history / by Alan N. Kay.
        p. cm.
    Includes bibliographical references.
    Summary: After the sale of her mother at a slave auction tears apart her family, Lisa runs away to avoid the same fate.
    ISBN 1-57249-208-2 (alk. paper)
    1. Underground railroad--Juvenile fiction. [1. Underground railroad--Fiction. 2. Fugitive slaves--Fiction. 3. Slavery--Fiction. 4. Afro-Americans--Fiction.] I. Title.

PZ7.K178 Se 2000
[Fic]--dc21

00-043442

PRINTED IN THE UNITED STATES OF AMERICA

This series is dedicated to my wonderful parents. To my beautiful mother whose love of reading and trips to the library instilled an appreciation and a desire to read and learn that still burns within me today. And to my awesome father whose commitment and dedication to my education allowed me to succeed as a teacher, historian, and author.

Thank you.

Contents

Characters

Lisa—a 12-year-old slave girl on a rice plantation in Georgia
Jack—her father, also a slave
Mr. Jones—their owner
David Adams—a 12-year-old Irish boy in Boston, Massachusetts

David's family
Jonathan Adams—David's father
Regina Adams—David's mother
William—David's grandpa, Regina's father
Thomas, Mary, and Helen—David's younger brother and sisters
George—David's cousin
Uncle Sean—George's father, Jonathan Adams' younger brother
Uncle Robert—David's other uncle, his father's older brother
Aunt Patricia—Uncle Robert's wife
Joshua, Zachary, Ethan, Rachel and Jamie—David's other cousins, children of Uncle Robert and Aunt Patricia

The following characters existed in real life and play roles similar to what they really did.
Mrs. Woodhouse—a free black schoolteacher in Savannah, Georgia
Francis Ellen Watkins Harper—a free black writer and speaker against slavery (friends with the famous Frederick Douglass)
Mr. F. H. Pettis—a New York lawyer who specialized in capturing runaway slaves

Mr. John Coburn—a free black anti-slavery organizer and
  fighter living in Boston

Mr. William C. Nell—a white anti-slavery writer who works in
  Boston (friends with the famous William Lloyd Garrison)

*Special note: Anti-slavery people were known as abolition-
ists. They organized, spoke out, and actively tried to end
slavery in any way they could.*

Preface

What is historical fiction and who are the Young Heroes of History?

Young Heroes of History focuses on children and young adults who were heroes in their time. Although they may not have achieved fame or fortune, they made a difference in the lives of those near to them. Many were strong in body and spirit, but others managed to do the best they could in the time and place in which they lived.

Although the heroes of this series are fictional, these young Americans are placed in situations that were very real. The events of the time period as well as many of the people in these stories are accurately based on the historical records. Sometimes the language and actions of the people may be hard to understand or may seem inappropriate, but this was a different time. This format allows readers to experience history and not just read about history.

Chapter One

The Escape

Everyone was staring and laughing and pointing at her. No matter which way Lisa's mother turned there was some stranger looking her body over. She wanted to run. She wanted to hide. She wanted to cover her almost naked body or at least to look away, but they wouldn't let her. She was surrounded.

The man to her left banged a mallet on his podium.

"Who'll start the bidding on this beautiful young nigger?" he called to the men in the room.

The men all looked at each other nervously wondering who would start and with how much. It was always a mind game at these slave auctions. If you started too high, you might end up paying too much, but if you started too low, too many buyers would jump in and run the price up even more. It all depended on who wanted slaves that day and what slaves were available.

Today, there were only about 30 men in the room. Some were standing in the back but most were seated on makeshift chairs or propped up boxes. A few well-dressed gentlemen circled around, looking at the slaves who were still to be sold, pointing and making notes. One man who walked with a limp was staring wickedly at the women, his mouth hung open and his tongue halfway out. He sweated like a mule and chuckled to himself as he slowly walked past. He stopped directly in front of Lisa and smiled a large toothless smile. Then, he breathed heavily and moved on to the platform where Lisa's mother stood standing partly clothed and chained like an animal. His smile grew even wider and his left hand slowly started to rub his chest.

"How old is she?" he asked the auctioneer.

"Twenty-eight years old," the auctioneer answered in a loud voice so everyone would hear, "just the right age for all kinds of field work."

"Or maybe some other kinda work!" someone yelled out. The crowd laughed in a deep, raspy voice.

"She certainly looks strong enough for it!"

More laughter.

"Let's see her backside," another called out.

Lisa closed her eyes to hold back the tears. She wanted to scream. Why were they doing this? Who were these men who treated them like sideshow dogs and laughed at their pain? Why did they think it was funny and why were they taking away her mother? What would they do with her? And where was her daddy? Couldn't they just leave her alone?

"Please, gentlemen," the auctioneer interrupted, "what is the starting bid?"

"I'll start with $100," the man with the limp slurred as he looked up at Lisa's half-naked mother.

"Oh my God!" Lisa cried to herself in a panic. Her body started to shake, her lips began to quiver, and her stomach was in knots. "That monster wants my mother!"

"Two hundred," someone else shouted.

The man with the limp turned around to see who bid.

"Two fifty," he said angrily.

"Three hundred!"

"What do you mean three hundred?" the man shot back angrily. "That nigger is mine!"

"Now just a minute sir," the auctioneer interrupted.

"Don't 'just a minute me,'" the man yelled back. "I want that nigger, you hear. I need that nigger. She's just the kinda woman I been looking for: young and pretty, not too many scars on her. She'll make me a fine addition to my little family."

He looked again at Lisa's mother, smiled greedily, and turned around.

"Three fifty!"

Silence.

Lisa prayed that someone would do something. She even hoped someone would quickly buy her mother. Anything was better than to be sold to this man. He was the kind of man who only wanted her mother so he could use her body for whatever he felt like doing. Lisa had heard the stories. Even though she was only 10, her mother had told her of the awful things that many masters do to their slave women. They were the master's property and they could do what they liked with them.

"Sold for $350!" the auctioneer yelled as he banged his gavel on the podium. "Take her away sir."

"No, no," Lisa cried aloud.

"Don't worry little girl," the man said as he approached Lisa's mother. "I'll take good care of her."

"No, no!" Lisa cried again. She tried to run but her feet wouldn't move the chains. The man stepped up onto the platform and smiled again at Lisa's mother as his eyes looked up and down her body.

"Yeah, you'll do just fine," he said as he pulled out a neck iron.

Before Lisa's mother knew what was happening to her, the brace was around her neck like a dog on a leash and the man was pulling her out the door.

"No, no!" she cried. "Let me say good-bye to my baby. Please, please! Lisa!"

"Mommy, mommy!" Lisa cried. "Don't go! Someone help her, please someone stop him. Mommy!"

Lisa screamed and screamed and screamed; then she woke up with a fright. She was panting hard and her heart was beating so loud she felt it would burst through her ribs.

"Oh that nightmare again," she said softly. "When will it end? When will I stop being afraid?"

Lisa's head suddenly hit something hard. She was abruptly knocked from her thoughts and thrown back into reality. She opened her eyes wide. The image of the evil man dragging her mother away was still in front of her. She closed her eyes and shivered. She opened them again. The image was fading but it was still dark.

It had been almost three years now since Lisa had last seen her mother and still she had those terrible nightmares of her mother being sold away. Lisa and her father had heard nothing from her. For all Lisa knew she was dead, but Lisa couldn't help but hope that some day she would see her mother again. Fortunately, no one at the auction that day was interested in a girl as young as Lisa, so she was allowed to return to her daddy at the plantation. Her master promised that as soon as she was old enough he would try to sell her again. He'd had enough of her mother's lip and he would soon see that all the females in Lisa's family had been sold away. From that day on, Lisa lived every day in fear of being sold away from her daddy and never seeing the people she loved again.

Lisa suddenly coughed. Something fluffy was on her face. She blew air on her nose. The fluff was still there. She coughed and blew again and began to wake up more. Opening her eyes a third time she saw only darkness and felt the soft cotton all around her. She tried to stretch her legs and arms but they knocked against hard wood. The sound reminded her that she was hiding in an oak box on a ship that her father said would finally take her away from the fear of slavery and into freedom. She'd been in that box, legs crunched up, arms hugging her waist, covered in cotton, for two days now.

She'd only seen her daddy once, the day before, when he came to change the cotton and give her some bread and water. He was afraid that if he did not change the cotton, then the other sailors on board would begin to notice the smell of Lisa's waste.

"The only good thing about so little food," Lisa thought, "was that she had not had to go the bathroom since her dad had changed the cotton. Only the urine had mixed in with the cotton and once that had dried it didn't bother her."

Her legs were beginning to ache again though. Yesterday, they had gone completely numb but now the blood was beginning to flow back and a deep throbbing began in her foot and traveled all the way up her thigh to her hips.

"When will this be over?"she cried to herself as her mind drifted back to when her escape from the horrors of slavery finally began.

Her father had only told her. "It's time, Lisa," when he took her by the hand and casually began to walk away from the rice patties and into the woods that Saturday afternoon. Then, once they were out of sight of the plantation, he told her to run and run and run and to not look back.

They ran all day and half the night. Never once did they go near a road and whenever they heard a dog bark, her daddy's head whipped around to see if the hounds were after them. Then, he'd grab her hand and run deeper into the woods. Lisa never even got a chance to ask her daddy a question. He'd either shush her or she would be so out of breath she couldn't even speak. Instead her mind whipped up images of blood-hounds catching up to them, biting them, chewing on them until the slave catchers found them and dragged what was left of them back to the plantation. She ran faster and faster.

Finally, when they could run no further, they stopped and lay in some grass. Daddy gathered up some rocks and branches and lay them in a circle to try to keep any snakes or other animals away. They didn't dare light a fire. Fortunately, the summer night was more than warm enough. As long as the mosquitos didn't eat them alive or some poisonous snake decide to come for a visit they might make it through the night.

"But what would the day bring?" Lisa thought. They obviously were running away and Lisa knew better than to ask her daddy any questions. She had once talked with her daddy about running away but he had told her that it was not something that they should discuss. He had known other slaves who had been caught running away, or even talking about it, and they had been whipped or sold or sometimes even killed. Besides, if they one day did run away it would be better if he kept it a secret to make sure no one stopped them.

"Go to sleep, Lisa," her daddy reminded her. "You're gonna need your rest for tomorrow."

The next day brought more of the same. The plantation was approximately 20 miles south of Savannah, so it was not difficult to get close to the city even with the many detours they had taken around streams, fallen trees, and the occasional alligator. They didn't have to worry about getting lost. Many slaves had ran into the woods just to get away for a short time. They had spread the word as to where to go and where to hide. Unfortunately for Lisa, her daddy did not think it was wise to sneak into Savannah on a Sunday. So even though they were just outside the city, they would have to spend one more night in the forest. Better to try to enter the city on a busy Monday than on any other day, Lisa's daddy had told her.

When they finally walked into downtown Savannah, it was already late Monday morning. Soon, the overseer at the plantation would know that they had escaped and it wouldn't take long for them to start looking in the city.

"Walk like you know what you are doing," her daddy said as he grabbed her hand and tugged her along. "They won't bother us if we look like we are supposed to be here."

The city was filled with noises and sights that Lisa had not seen in several years. The last time she had been there was when her father needed some help because old Nick was sick. She found it almost impossible not to lift her head and gaze wide-eyed at all the activity around her. People and horses were everywhere and they all seemed to have a place to go. Some horses pulled carriages while others had single riders on their backs. Businessmen dressed in black suits and ladies in their fancy gowns walked amidst sailors, merchants, and other workers going about their business. A woman was yelling at her little boy who was running down the wide dirt street. There were plenty of black people too. Some of them, her daddy had told her, were even free and she could tell now that this must be so because they seemed to walk differently, like they had a purpose, like they weren't doing a job for someone else but for themselves.

Even the air was different, Lisa noticed, as her nose wrinkled with the smells of smoke from the fireplaces and the mills. Pigeons flew around everywhere dropping their loads on buildings and people alike, while the horses added their own large craps to the unique smells of this strange city.

The buildings were built of brick or wood. They all seemed to be at least three to four stories tall and many were covered with beautiful green vines that grew up the walls. Beyond the buildings, Lisa could see the masts of many sailing ships sticking up into the sky, some even higher than the buildings. As she realized that they were headed towards the waterfront she became more excited.

"Daddy, are we taking a boat?" she exclaimed.

"Ssshhhh," he replied. "Just keep walking."

Lisa looked at all the many boats in the river. There were small ships with only one sail, bigger ships with several sails, and even some huge ships with three or four large masts reaching up into the sky. The sailors were busy throwing things on or off the ships, yelling at each at other, and climbing up and down the masts as easily as if they were monkeys climbing trees. Lisa dragged her heels trying to watch all the activity while her father kept pulling at her.

"C'mon, Lisa," he grumbled, "if we don't hurry, we'll miss our appointment."

Up ahead, Lisa saw a small black boy stop suddenly, look around the street to see if anyone was watching him, and enter into a yard through a gate. When her daddy stopped in front of the same gate and led Lisa through it, she grew even more excited as she realized that the adventure was really getting sneaky and tricky now. They turned in the yard, approached a door in the back, and walked into the kitchen.

"Hello there, Jack!" an older black woman cried as she threw her arms around him and squeezed him like they were long lost friends. "And this must be little Lisa. How are you, girl?"

"Fine, ma'am," Lisa replied politely.

"Lisa, this is Mrs. Woodhouse," her father began, quickly shutting the door behind him. "She teaches free black children to read and write and do all kinds of things, and this is her school."

"Wow!" Lisa said as she looked around the strangely decorated room. It appeared to be a kitchen, complete with a stove, several cabinets, and a countertop to cut food on. But, in the middle of the room were several desks with small chalkboards. The few children in the room were getting their books out of the paper bags which they used to hide their books as they walked through the streets of Savannah. Mrs. Woodhouse was smiling in front of Lisa and watching the students unpack their things. Her broad grin surprised Lisa because of the beautiful teeth she had. Everyone she had ever known on the plantation had missing or bent teeth and their smiles were often awkward. Her clothes were even strange. She looked more like a white woman dressed in respectable clothes with the collar buttoned all the way to her neck and a pretty pink bow-tie around her waist. She was holding a walking cane in her left hand which she used to sturdy her slightly bent frame.

"Come, come you two," she suddenly said as she pushed them into a small, dark room off to the side of the kitchen. "There is no need to discuss this in front of the children. You two stay in here for a little while. I will be back shortly after I start the lesson."

"Daddy, daddy," Lisa began as Mrs. Woodhouse quietly closed the door, "what's going on? Who are those children? What is this place? What are we gunna do? What about..."

"Calm down, calm down, girl," her daddy began with a laugh. "Just have a seat over there and I'll explain what I can."

Lisa sat down in a small, padded wooden chair in the corner and was distracted for a moment by the softness of the pillowed cushions.

"That nice lady there," her father began in a whisper, pointing towards the kitchen, "is a fine educated free black woman, and she is gunna help us!"

Lisa's eyes grew wide and her jaw dropped slightly. She waited patiently for her daddy to continue although she was so excited she could hardly keep her seat in the chair. "You see," her daddy finally said, "I met her one day on one of my many travels here to Savannah for Mr. Jones. We wuz both sittin' in the Bryan Baptist Church which, by the way, is a fine black church, built by our people for our people, when I happened to notice that she was reading the Bible real good. Well, I started talkin' to her and I find out that she is free and she is a widow and that she has been helpin' little free black children ta learn. So, I went and started askin' her about being free and all kinds of things. We kinda struck up a friendship, so I kept on seeing her whenever I came to Savannah. Pretty soon, she agreed to help me find a way up north so we could be free."

"Ohhhh my, praise the Lord, Daddy!" Lisa cried as she fell to the floor on her knees in prayer. "We gunna be free, free! Oh thank you, Jesus, thank you."

"Now calm down, girl," her daddy said not too seriously. He had a huge grin on his face and found it hard to be stern with Lisa now. "We need to be quiet here. This is a wonderful thing that is happening, but it is also a dangerous thing. You know what can happen to us, but you also must remember what can happen to people like Mrs. Woodhouse who help us. If anyone finds out, she could be sent to prison, or a mob could hang her, and I don't want to even think about that."

"I'm sorry, Daddy," Lisa said as she got up off her feet, wiped her tears, and sat back down in the chair. "I'm just so excited. No more living in fear! No more wondering if we gunna be together. We gunna be free!"

"I know, I know," he said with a laugh as he walked across the room and gave Lisa a big hug. Even though Lisa was growing up fast she still was smaller than her daddy and when they hugged, his arms wrapped around her head and brought her into his huge chest. She loved the warm feeling of his strong arms around her body, protecting her from the world. On cool autumn evenings, his furry chest would be like a soft pillow and she could hug him like that for hours.

That night, a ship's captain had arrived at Mrs. Woodhouse's. She explained that he was a friend of hers and that he had once promised to help slaves escape up north if she ever knew of one in need. Unfortunately, he didn't count on two slaves at once. Lisa's daddy, Jack, they decided, could pose as a sailor on the ship. It was not uncommon for blacks, both slave and free, to work as sailors. Since this plan of theirs had been going on for some time now, Jack had been busy watching the boats, talking to the people at the docks, and trying to find out as much as he could about how to be a sailor. It wouldn't be too hard to fit him in as a member of the crew. It was Lisa who would be the problem.

A young black girl would arouse suspicion especially on a sailing ship where women were considered bad luck. The sailors would have no problem with Jack but there is no way they would accept any story for Lisa. She would have to be smuggled. Several months ago, Jack had come up with the idea of shipping her in a box disguised as a personal gift to a friend. Mrs. Woodhouse knew someone in Baltimore where they could ship the box to and they could tell everyone that the box was a special present that could only be opened upon delivery. In June, Jack had managed to gather some old, discarded cotton off the plantation to cushion the box and then bring it to Mrs. Woodhouse's address. The captain had agreed to the plan and all that they needed was a weekend after the planting when they would have the time to make their escape.

It sounded like a wonderful plan at the time to Lisa, but now that she was sitting in the dark, with her stomach churning, and her arms and legs locked in pain, she wished that maybe she was back home in the rice fields.

The sound of a footstep brought Lisa to attention. Were they in Baltimore already?

Bangs and crashes suddenly shattered the silence. Someone was throwing boxes around and yelling all kinds of terrible things.

"Where is that damned thing," the voice said. "I can't go anywhere without it. I know it's here somewhere."

Suddenly, Lisa's head banged the side of the box as a corner of it was lifted.

"What the hell's in this box?" the voice said. "Damn thing's heavy as a load of rocks."

Lisa's head was still ringing when the box got lifted again and her arm smashed into the side.

"Oh Lord, oh Lord," Lisa cried to herself in the blackness. "Don't let him find me."

"I'll never find it with this box in the way," the voice said.

Lisa's legs fell to the side, her arms flailed about, and her head smashed into the top of the box. All of her weight was pressing on her head when she realized that she was upside down. Her neck was slightly bent as she tried to support her weight. Thankfully the way she had turned allowed her shoulders to support some of her weight as well. Otherwise, she felt as if her neck would have broken under the awful strain. Thank goodness for the cotton providing some comfort to her head.

"There it is!" the voice yelled. "I thought I'd never find it. Damn thing is always rolling somewhere. I'd better go see if I can find me some..."

As the voice trailed off, Lisa realized that the man had found what he was looking for but was not going to put her box back the right way. She wanted to cry out to him but she knew she couldn't do that. She began to panic. The blood was rushing to her head and making her dizzy. She could feel her insides all weighing down on her. Her breathing became shallow and she choked on some cotton.

"Daddy," she whispered through tears, "help me."

Sometime later (Lisa had no idea how long she had been upside down because she had passed out), Lisa awakened when the box suddenly threw her to the side again. Her head hit the boards, her arms banged the edges, and her legs twisted underneath her. With a loud thud she was upright again.

"Daddy?" she whispered to herself.

Three soft taps on the top: that meant it was Daddy! Then she heard the creaky sounds of wood being pried open. Light poured into the box and then a large black hand came through

the cotton, grabbed her under the arm, and pulled her gently
out of the box.

"Lisa honey, are you O.K.?" her daddy whispered to her.
Lisa was still disoriented and dizzy. Her eyes were hurt
by the light and her muscles were frozen.

"I'm fine, Daddy," she said as her legs fell out from under her and she collapsed into her daddy's arms. "I'm just a
little dizzy from being upside down is all."

"You're such a brave girl," Daddy said as he helped support her weight. "And I was so worried about you when I saw
old Ben go down into the hold. He was looking for his good
luck stone he had dropped again. Thank goodness he didn't
find you."

"No, he didn't find me but he did manage to turn me
upside down and leave me there," Lisa replied in an annoyed
voice. "How much longer do I have to do this, Daddy?"

"Only a couple more days," he said. "The captain has a
little business to do but he wants to get to Baltimore as soon
as possible and get rid of us."

"Hey Jack, what are you doing down there?" a voice said
suddenly.

Lisa and Jack turned to see a small sailor looking right at
them. It was Tom, the first mate, and he had been no friend
of Jack's since day one. He obviously did not like blacks and
he liked them even less on his ship. Fortunately, at least until
now, Jack had managed to steer clear of him.

"Uh, I was just uh, I was just uh," Jack stuttered.

"Who's that?" Tom asked, stepping forward with his lantern to see Lisa standing next to Jack.

Every possible excuse Jack came up with ahead of time
whirled through his mind but each one seemed ridiculous
now. His mind raced. He couldn't run. He couldn't hide. He
could try to kill him. But no, he couldn't do that.

"She's my daughter," Jack said slowly. "She was hiding in
this here box and..."

"Your daughter?" Tom exclaimed. "Your daughter? You
got a nigger girl on board this ship? Wait 'til I tell the captain!"

Tom turned around and headed towards the ladder to take him above deck, but before he got more than two steps a large piece of wood came crashing down on his head.

"I hated to do that," Jack said, still holding the club. "But I didn't know what else to do."

"Oh, Daddy," Lisa cried, "what are we gunna do now? Everyone will find out and we'll be sent back or killed or thrown overboard or maybe they'll sell us down South!"

"Hold on, hold on, honey," her daddy interrupted. "We ain't gunna do no such thing, you hear? I'll think of something. Here, you'd best get back in that box. I'll take him to the captain and maybe we'll figure out something together. Now don't you worry."

He began to motion Lisa back into the box.

"But, Daddy," Lisa whined.

"Git," he said sternly.

"Oooohhh."

Lisa stepped into the box and sat down on the cotton again. She curled up her legs and hugged her chest as she waited for her daddy to close up the box.

"Oh, I almost forgot, here's some water and some bread," her daddy said as he reached down into the box to hand it to her. "It's not as much as last time cuz the others are wondering why I am eating so much. Now don't worry dear, everything will be alright. You just rest in there and I'll take care of everything."

He leaned into the box, kissed Lisa on the forehead, then began piling the cotton up over her head. The cover was placed on tight and everything was black again.

Chapter Two

The Irish

"C-c-crackkk," the ball went straight up in the air. George watched it go right towards the space between first and second base.

"Run, George, run!" David yelled.

George ran as hard as he could to first. He still couldn't believe he hit it towards the outfield. It was the first time all day he'd had a hit and the first time in months that he'd ever hit one of John O'Malley's blazing pitches.

"Yeah, nice hit!" His cousin David called again. "Stay right there, Georgie, and I'll hit you home, no problem."

"Yeah, well, we'll just see about that, Southie," John called to David. He'd given David that nickname four months ago when he realized that David did not live in the slums of Boston's Fort Hill or the North End as most of his Irish buddies did. Instead, David lived with his uncles and aunt in the "respectable" areas of South Boston where the Irish were not welcome.

The nickname really bothered David because it was a constant reminder to him that he was an outsider to his fellow Irish as much as he was among the neighborhood boys of the South End. As an Irish boy in a non-Irish neighborhood David wasn't given a chance. To the Germans, English, French and other "real" Americans he was just a stupid Irish immigrant who belonged with the rest of his kind in the slums and at the bottom of the heap. Even the niggers, they would joke at him, were better than the Irish.

David stepped up to the plate. He wouldn't let John or any other boy get the most of him, whether he was Irish or German or French or whatever. He and his cousin George had worked hard to find friends in Fort Hill despite John's teasings and taunts, and it was only here on the baseball field that David truly could prove he was anyone's equal.

The boys had been playing baseball on the Common ever since they first heard about the new sport. Although they had never seen a real game, they knew all the rules and they had enough players. All they needed was a field to play in and the Common was the obvious choice. It was hundreds of yards wide and almost a quarter mile long, with grass fields and walking paths crossing in every direction. On beautiful summer days like this one, the Common was a natural place to play and even though they were constantly run off by the local Boston Police, they usually got in several innings every game.

"South-eee, South-eee," the boys in the outfield began to taunt. "South-eee is an easy out, Southie is an easy out."

David's hands gripped the bat tighter. The taunts never bothered him when he was at bat. He knew he was a good hitter. He was one of the best hitters on the team. He'd already hit one home run today and now with his cousin George on base for the first time in weeks, he had lots of good reasons to hit another.

"Strike one," the umpire called before David realized the pitch had been thrown.

"Whoops, I'd better pay attention," he thought.

"Stee-rike two."

David's hands began to sweat now.

"C'mon, David," George yelled, "you can do it, hit me home!"

"South-eee," the taunts began again.

David just stared right at John who looked a little nervous despite the two strikes. This wouldn't be the first time that David had a hit after two strikes. John looked down at the ball, rubbed his hands all over it, and wound up.

"Fast ball," David thought suddenly. "It's a fast ball. John always does that before a fast ball."

"C-c-craackkk!" the ball went soaring over John's head, towards the street.

"Yeahhhh!" David's teammates cried out as David dropped the bat and made his way to first. George was already rounding second and the ball was still in the air. The outfielders were running to get the ball. David's team was cheering. It looked like another home run!

David's foot barely touched first as he swung around and headed towards second. He looked up to see where the ball was and then his heart sank. Standing right in the spot where the ball was rolling to was a group of boys from David's neighborhood. He even knew the boy who was bending down to pick up the ball. It was Russell, the boy from down the street.

David's feet slowly stopped, the cheering quickly ended, and all eyes looked towards the new group of boys. There were at least 9 or 10 of them and they were all older than David and his Irish friends.

"Nice hit," Russell said, walking into the field and tossing the ball casually into David's hands. "Not bad for an Irishman."

"Thanks," David replied awkwardly.

"But hey," Russell continued. "Shouldn't you good little Catholic boys be in church?"

The other boys with Russell began to laugh.

"In fact," he went on, "I definitely remember telling you the last time we saw you that the Common ain't for Irish."

"It's for everybody," David shot back.

"No. It. Ain't," Russell returned, pointing his finger into David's chest with every word. "It's for Americans!"

"We are Americans!" David yelled back.

"No you ain't. You don't talk like us, you don't work like us, you don't smell like us, and you don't even pray like us. You Irish ain't never been Americans. You stay walled up in your ugly, smelly slums, you don't wanna go to our schools, you drink and beg and rob and steal. My dad says that before you came, Boston was a nice, decent place where you could walk outside and not have to worry about your safety."

"Yeah, well we wouldn't have to live in these slums if you gave us a decent job," John piped in. "My dad ain't never had a steady job since he got here. You won't let him. All the good jobs are for 'real' Americans, everyone tells him, and there was even those ads in the paper with the 'no Irish need apply' signs."

"If that's so," Russell said, pointing his thumb in a sideways manner towards David, "then what about old David and George here? Their family has got jobs."

"That's cuz David's mom felt sorry for his dad and gave him a chance," John answered. "Besides, he ain't real Irish anyhow. How can he be when his dad's a Catholic and his mom's a uni...uni whatever that's called."

"Unitarian," George threw in.

"Whatever," Russell said. "Anyhow, that ain't the point. The point is that I told you that this Common ain't for you and I meant it. Now you better go or me and the others will have to do something about it."

"No!" David shouted. "You can't make us. There is plenty of room for everyone."

"Not for you, twerp," Russell said as he pushed David in the chest, making him stumble backwards.

"Hey," George yelled, running towards his cousin. "You can't do that! Leave him alone."

"Try and stop us," Russell said defiantly.

George looked up at Russell's huge body and knew that he was in trouble. George was only 10 years old and David was only 12, while Russell and his friends were 13, 14, and 15. Even John, the biggest Irish kid there, was only 13 and he was nowhere near as big as Russell.

"You bastard!" George screamed as he ran toward Russell. He wasn't much taller than Russell's waist, but the sudden impact threw Russell off balance.

"Get off me, you little punk," Russell yelled, as he kicked George off him with a shrug.

"Get them!" he yelled again.

Everything went crazy as the bigger boys jumped on the Irish kids. There were more of the Irish kids so some of them didn't get grabbed. Those who were caught put up a hard fight, but they were no match for the bigger kids. David, John, and George were grabbed first since they were so close while John managed to hold his own for a few minutes.

Russell grabbed David and swung him around by the back of the shirt. He let go and David went flying to the ground. George, who had been ignored because of his size, caught Russell by surprise and punched him in the stomach.

"Oooofff," Russell groaned as he let out a gasp of air.

He turned towards George, but David tackled him from behind.

Meanwhile, John had been fist fighting with another boy nearby. He had managed to hit the older boy in the nose and blood was running down his face.

"You little creep," he spat through the blood.

The boy kept his fists up near his face, protecting his nose, but he continued to back up as John pressed his attack. Without watching where he was going, the boy tripped backwards over the fallen Russell, David and George and all the boys became a jumble of bodies. John grabbed David's and George's hands, shouting, "Let's get outta here!"

All the Irish boys ran. Screaming and yelling, they knocked people out of their way as they tried to escape. The Common was filled with people. Several times, someone was pushed down or swung around, but no one was seriously hurt. The chase lasted for a few minutes, but the Irish boys were able to weave through the crowd. Finding themselves at the edge of the Common, they bent down holding their knees and breathing hard.

"We, we made it," one of the boys said.

"Yeah, good fighting, John," someone else said.

"I certainly let him have it, huh?" John said with a grin.

"Yeah, nice punch," added David. "Thanks for the save."

"Yeah, well, no problem," John said awkwardly. "You may be a Southie, but you're still an Irishman. Besides, you and your cousin stood up pretty well to that big doofus."

"Thanks," George said eagerly.

"Yeah, well don't think too much of it," John said to George, all friendliness in his voice gone again.

"Hey, look where we are," another boy said.

"Yeah, we're right by the hill," added another.

The boys looked around to see the fine houses of Beacon Hill standing tall amidst the sunshine and the trees. These houses were nothing less than mansions, the boys felt, and only the very best of the city lived there. They were all several stories tall, made of strong beautifully painted wood with various colors of shutters around the windows. Some of the houses had dark green ivy growing up the side and across the walls. They were all tightly packed together in a row, but it was easy to see where one house ended and another began because each house had a distinct color and design that made it stand out from the ones around it. They stood in a neat row that went all the way up Beacon Street along the Common. Here was the best view of the city anywhere.

"That's where all the money is," one boy said.

"And all the power," said another.

"Not like we'll ever know what that's like," said John.

"What's that supposed to mean?" David asked.

"Figures you'd say that, Southie," John answered. "You don't know what it's like to be a true Irishman, living where you live."

"Let's not start that again, John," said Frederick, another boy who lived near John. "I'm tired of picking on those two. Besides, David's a great hitter and I like having him on my team."

"Yeah fine," John answered. "But we still would'a won if those boys hadn't shown up."

"Hey," little Bobby chimed in, "ain't the niggers live on the other side of the hill?"

"Yeah they do," David answered.

"Let's go see!" Bobby said excitedly.

"We can't, dummy," John answered. "You know how a group of 12 Irish boys wandering through a nigger neighborhood would look? We'd get so many stares and people would start saying things and pretty soon I'm sure there'd be trouble."

"Well, O.K.," Bobby answered. "But can't we just go near?"

"Yeah, John," Frederick added, "why don't we go a little closer, maybe we'll even see a few of the little darkies."

"Heh-heh," John laughed. "Well O.K., we can cut around these nice houses. I've always wanted to see them up close."

The boys wandered up Beacon Street, cuttting through an alley that took them further up the hill. When they were almost near the top, David suddenly stopped and said, "Hey, guys, wait a second, go through this alley here."

"How do you know about this?" Frederick asked.

"Uhhhh," David said awkwardly, "there's a kid in my school who's black. I sit next to him sometimes and he told me about this here secret alley."

"You got a nigger in your school?" Bobby asked wide-eyed.

"Well, yeah sure," David replied, "they let the Negroes into the regular schools three years ago, remember?"

"No," Bobby answered plainly, "I was too little then, plus I never went to school in the first place."

"You and George are the only ones who've gone to school," John added. "That's another thing that makes you different."

"Well, it's not like it costs anything," George said.

"It's a waste of time!" John shouted back, obviously this was a sore spot for him. "Besides we're all too busy working to help our families for any stupid school."

"C'mon, c'mon," Frederick quickly interrupted, he didn't want to have this argument again, "we need to get in the alley before someone sees us."

The boys walked quietly into the alley. It was very dark despite the full sun. On each side of the alley was the outside brick wall of a house. The boys noticed right away how cool it was in the alley and how many little crevices and hiding spots there were in the walls. As they walked two by two (it was only wide enough for two of them at a time) they would suddenly see a door or a turnoff. It was like a maze. David whispered down the line that these alleys were where the Negroes ran when they were trying to escape from the slave catchers.

"Hey, you're not friends with this nigger, are you?" John suddenly asked.

"No...no, of course not," David answered.

"Good," John quickly replied, "cuz I know what a nigger lover your mom is."

"Yeah, well I ain't," David answered. "How could I be like my parents? They went and left us here in Boston while they went off to Kansas to 'save the world for the free soil' as they say."

"Why do your parents care so much for the niggers anyway," Bobby asked softly.

"I dunno," David answered. "They've always been that way. My mom used to come home every week from her church and tell us how her preacher told of the evils of slavery. I listened, but I didn't care much cuz it wasn't like I could do anything about it."

"What about your dad?" Frederick asked.

"Oh, he'd really try to get involved," David said. "I guess maybe he was trying to prove something, but he was more into it than my mom. He would go to meetings and disappear sometimes and then come back as if nothing had happened. My mom knew where he went, but she would never tell us."

"Didn't his boss get upset?" John said.

"Didn't seem to," David replied. "I think the whole group of them was into this abolitionist stuff."

A door suddenly opened. The boys froze. A woman stepped out into the alley and walked straight ahead. Fortunately, she didn't seem to notice them. She was preoccupied with what she was doing, and the boys were able to crouch back in an alcove and watch.

"What's she doin'?" Bobby whispered.

"She's hanging up her laundry," John answered. "Keep quiet and I think she'll be done soon."

The boys watched as the woman took out several pairs of pants, shirts, and socks, hanging them up carefully on the clothesline. She was singing a song that none of them recognized and was so caught up in what she was doing that the boys were able to whisper a little.

"That shirt is just my size," John whispered.

"So?" interjected Frederick.

"So, I'm thinking maybe I should 'borrow' it," answered John in a nasty voice.

"You can't do that!" Bobby almost shouted. David put his hand over Bobby's mouth to hold back the noise but Bobby shook his face free. "You know the code, what everybody says: laundry is untouchable. It's something that we all must leave alone and respect."

"Yeah, but that don't apply to niggers," John said.

"Why not?" David asked.

"What do you mean, 'why not?'" John said. "They're niggers. You know, the bottom of the barrel, the end of line."

"My dad says we Irish are the bottom of the barrel," Bobby said in a low tone. "He says we must be, otherwise they wouldn't treat us so."

"Yeah, but he's not including the niggers," Frederick interrupted. "The niggers ain't even in the barrel."

"But they have better jobs and better houses than we do," Bobby said again.

"That's cuz they let them," Frederick replied. "These abolitionists feel sorry for them and they make the whole city go crazy making sure the nigger gets his fair share while they let us rot in our slums."

"It ain't that simple," David interrupted. "They got to live in fear all the time. Imagine if any day some stranger could grab you and take you to the South saying that you were a runaway slave. They can't prove they are free and the judge gets more money if he says they are guilty than if they are free."

"That one of your mother's speeches?" John said in a sarcastic tone. "You sound just like a preacher."

David didn't answer. He wasn't sure if he was upset because John ignored his comment or because he *did* sound like his mother.

"I'm gonna get me some of those nice shirts," John said as he started to get up. The woman had finished what she was doing and was heading back into her house.

"Don't!" David almost shouted, he was still afraid of someone hearing them.

"Why not, nigger lover?" John asked. "That one of your friend's houses?"

"No, of course not," David replied nervously. "It's just that it's wrong."

"We already went through that," John said in an annoyed tone. "Now the rest of you with me?"

John looked around.

"Fred?" he asked.

"Sure, why not," Fred answered as he too got up and stood next to John. The rest of the boys began to stand up.

"I certainly ain't no nigger lover," David's cousin George said as he stood up quickly. David looked at George in surprise, then David turned and noticed that he was the only one still squatting.

"Well," John said towards David. "You coming or are you really the Southie that I always said you wuz?"

"Of course I'm coming," David said as he quickly stood up. "I'm as Irish as you are."

"Good," John said, turning his back to David and facing the laundry hanging out to dry. "Let's go get some new clothes!"

Chapter Three

The Inspector

"What's going on here?" the captain said to Lisa's father, Jack. "Why are you here in my cabin this late at night, and why is my first mate asleep in your arms?"

"He's not asleep," Jack answered, laying the first mate down gently on the captain's bunk. "I had to knock him out."

"Knock him out? Why for God's sake?"

"He found out, sir," Jack said softly. "He caught me giving food to Lisa, my daughter."

"Oh, Lord," the captain said with a huge sigh, "I knew this might happen. And you had to get caught by him. Not only is he one of the best mates I've ever had, he also doesn't care too much for your people."

"Oh, I already noticed that, sir. I've tried to stay out of his way, but this time I couldn't."

"Well then, Jack, what am I supposed to do? Here I am the captain of the ship, my first mate is lying unconscious on my bed, and a fugitive slave is standing next to me with his daughter, a stowaway, on my ship."

Jack didn't answer. He still was not sure about this man. He had seemed friendly enough at Mrs. Woodhouse's, but once they set sail, he seemed to go out of the way to give Jack a hard time. Jack didn't know if he was just trying to provide a good cover for himself or if he really enjoyed treating Jack that way.

"Well, I could just arrest you," the captain said more to himself than to Jack. "That would be the safest thing to do."

"But s...sir," Jack spat out, his heart racing and his brow beginning to sweat, "what about the first mate? He knows you were sneaking me on board."

"Hhhhhhmmmm, well yes, that could present a problem. I don't fully trust him. If he could convince the authorities that I was involved, I would be ruined and he might be chosen as captain by the owners."

Jack's heart slowed down just a little.

"On the other hand," he continued, "there might also be a reward for you. I could offer to split it with him. That might keep him quiet."

Before the captain's thoughts could progress more towards that choice, Jack quickly interrupted.

"But, begging your pardon, sir, you just said you don't trust the man. He could claim you were smuggling me and still collect the reward. Then, he wouldn't have to share it with you and he would be the new captain."

Jack smiled a little to himself, hoping that this point he made would be enough.

"That's very true," the captain answered. "Maybe these abolitionists are right in what they say about you Negroes, you really are quite clever. Well then, what shall we do?"

Unfortunately, they had no more time to discuss the matter as the first mate began to groan and sit up.

"What happened?" he said, rubbing the back of his head. "I feel like I have been hit by a cannonball."

"You," he yelled, looking at Jack, "you're the nigger who hit me!"

"Captain, captain, sir," he said, swinging his legs to the floor and attempting to stand, "this nigger is hiding his daughter on board. I think he's a runaway and..."

"Hold on, hold on," the captain said as he caught the mate. His legs were still wobbly underneath him and if the captain had not caught him he would have fallen on the floor. "I know all this, Tom, and I appreciate what you've done, but this is more complicated than you realize."

Tom looked up at the captain, waiting for him to continue.

"You see, Tom," the captain finally went on, rubbing his chin and looking away nervously, "I know about this because I am responsible for it."

"What? You? But captain."

"I have always hated slavery," the captain went on. "It's a vile disgusting evil that embarrasses our country and insults our Lord. I have never had the bravery or the time to do anything more than despise it, so my life has not had much conflict in it. But, when I was approached to help bring this slave to freedom I realized that it was finally time that I do something."

"But you're breaking the law!"

"It's evil, Tom!" the captain shouted. "Don't you understand? The law means nothing in the face of this evil. Slave owners control the government and therefore the laws. Any law they write will only continue this immorality, and it is the duty of any God-fearing citizen to do anything in their power to stop it. And this is in my power."

"The only thing I understand, sir," the mate said bitterly, "is that you are breaking the law for this nigger."

"Alright, Tom, alright," the captain said, putting up his hands to stop Tom's protests. "Obviously you and I are on different sides of this issue, so let's make this simple. What are you going to do about it?"

"Well, sir, that's not my place to say," Tom said cautiously. He was obviously feeling the captain out to see what he would do.

"Yes, you're right about that," the captain returned. "So here's what I have to say. I suggest you keep this quiet. No one knows about this except you and me. I am going to drop them off at Baltimore and then we will be done with it."

"And what if I choose to discuss this matter with the authorities?"

"You, of course, have that choice," the captain answered. "But I would advise against it. If you do, I will make sure that you are implicated in this. I will claim that you were completely aware of the situation and indeed helped me conceal it from the men."

"That's a lie!" Tom shouted back.

"Of course it's a lie, but no one will know that. And you can continue to deny it. But even if you are let off, the doubt and questions that remain will ruin your career. What sailors will follow a mate or a captain that they don't know if they can trust?"

"Indeed, sir," Tom replied, looking the captain straight in the eyes. "What sailors will follow a captain that they don't trust?"

"Yes, I see your point, Tom, and here is what I will do in exchange for your silence. Since obviously you will no longer trust me, our relationship will need to end. However, you perhaps are unaware that the company is about to commission another ship. They might consider you for captain, and if I put in a good word for you then the ship will most certainly be yours, you will have your own crew, and you and I will never need to sail together again. However, if you challenge me on this, I will make sure that enough doubt remains that you will never get that ship and perhaps any ship ever."

Tom looked up at the captain, carefully considering what he had just heard. The room was still. The waves rolled against the ship. The wind howled against the sails. Each man's breath seemed to roar in the silence. Finally, the first mate stood up and faced the captain, his nose only two inches from the captain's.

"Alright, sir," Tom said through clenched teeth, "I'll go along with your *deal*, but in no way cuz I wanna help you or this nigger. I'm doing this for me and make no mistake. You and I are enemies and if I ever get the chance, I'll repay you for this, you can bet on it."

Tom stormed out of the captain's cabin and slammed the door behind him.

Lisa had no idea how much time was passing. Lack of food and the continuous darkness made her sleep most of the time. Her legs and arms had become permanently cramped and she had lost so much feeling in them that she couldn't even wiggle her toes or scratch her many itches. So when the box finally moved and woke Lisa out of her sleep, she was not sure if it had been one day or many since she last saw her father.

She could hear voices around her. She heard bangs and crashes. Obviously, something was going on. It sounded as if the boxes around her were being moved and that many men were down in the hold. From what she could hear, not one of the voices was her father's and that made her afraid.

"This one going?" said a voice.

"Yeah."

Lisa wasn't sure but the voice sounded like the man who had found her with her daddy the other day. She began to panic. What were they going to do? Maybe they would just throw the box in the ocean and she'd drown.

"Oh, Daddy, where are you?" she cried.

Lisa's head was thrown from side to side again as she felt the box being lifted and moved.

"Damn thing sure is heavy."

"Wait, let me adjust my hand."

Lisa was thrown backwards and up as the box was suddenly lifted and turned. The box landed on the main deck with a thud.

"What the heck is in there, Tom?" a sailor said to the first mate.

"Can't say," said Tom. "I'll just be glad when we're rid of it and on our way."

The other sailors looked at Tom, puzzled at his strange attitude about a box.

"It's just a box, Tom," Harry said, "not a relative. Where you want it?"

"Just throw it over there with the others for now," Tom answered. "The inspector will be here in a few minutes."

Harry and another sailor grabbed the box, throwing it a few feet against the side of the ship. As it landed, Tom chuckled to himself and turned away.

"That'll teach that nigger," he thought.

Sometime later (Lisa again was unsure how long because the toss across the ship had knocked her out again), voices outside the box woke Lisa.

"This one looks fine," said a voice, knocking on a box, "and so does this one."

"What's in here?" the voice said directly over Lisa's box.

"Just a personal gift for a citizen of Baltimore," Lisa heard the captain say.

"Open it please," said the voice.

"We really are in a hurry," the captain's voice said anxiously.

"Open it please," the voice repeated.

Lisa heard the box top being pried open again. Her heart began to race. What would she do?

Light began to appear from one of the corners. The lid was coming off.

"It really is supposed to be a surprise," the captain said.

"Yes, well maybe so," the voice continued, "but my job is to make sure that all items coming into Baltimore are legal and not a danger to the populace."

Lisa almost screamed. She could see the top of the box being moved around. Any second now and this man would see her head. Quickly, Lisa grabbed some cotton from under her legs and placed it above her. She knew it would make no difference, but she could think of nothing else to do.

"Mmmmm," the man groaned as he strained at the top.

A large white hand suddenly shot through the space between the top and the box itself. Then, the other hand grabbed the other side of the box. In seconds the lid would be off.

"What's going on?" she suddenly heard another voice interrupt. It was the first mate who found her.

"What was he going to do?" she thought fearfully.

The first mate approached the inspector who had taken his hand out of the box and was wiping it off.

"Just inspecting your boxes," the inspector said to Tom, "and who might you be?"

"Oh, I'm the first mate here," Tom replied, "although I won't be for long," he said as he looked over towards the captain.

"What's your interest in this box?" Tom asked.

"Nothing in particular," the inspector replied. "But it would not be the first time that something has been smuggled in a box labeled personal."

"Oh, I'm quite sure of that," Tom said.

The captain was getting nervous. He started walking towards the box and it was clear that Tom was enjoying watching the captain sweat.

"But, let me assure you," Tom continued with a sinister smile directed right at the captain. He put his hand on the inspector's back and turned him away, "this ship has nothing illegal that *I* am aware of. So if you don't mind we are in a hurry here. Harry, James, secure the cover on that box and let's get moving."

Chapter Four

The Pub

The doors of the pub burst open and a large figure stepped in.

"Sean Adams here?" the figure bellowed.

"Who wants to know?" Sean yelled from his barstool.

"Sergeant Johnson," the policeman called as he strode into the pub. He was dragging two boys with him as he walked. He held each of them by the ear making every effort to go as quickly as possible in order to cause the boys the most pain. They were holding his hands, trying to stop him, and shouting, "Let go, let go," as they dragged their feet.

Making his way around the tables and chairs, the officer noticed the crowd in the bar grow deathly quiet. Policemen were not an uncommon sight in Irish pubs and every time they showed up it meant trouble. The police felt it was their duty to protect the people of Boston from the drunken lunacy of the Irish, so they took it upon themselves to remind the Irish as much as possible that they were keeping an eye on them.

The Irish in the bar were always the first to admit that an Irishman loves to drink as much as, if not more than, the next man; however, they resented the police accusing them of being thieves and beggars because of it. The Irish claimed to be good, honest, decent, Catholic people, and if they ever committed crimes it was only the few rare exceptions when it was probably due to the conditions the Bostonians made them live in.

So, when Sergeant Johnson strode through the dark, crowded pub he was greeted by silent, unfriendly stares.

"This your boy?" he said, pulling George hard by the ear and shoving him in front of his father.

"Yeah."

"And this other one, your nephew?" he said, pulling David out as well.

"Yeah, what of it?" Sean asked.

"I caught them and a bunch of other boys running from the hill with this laundry in their hands. The others ran off, but I did manage to grab your son and nephew red-handed." The sergeant pulled out two shirts and a pair of socks that he had tucked in his back pockets.

"What?" Sean said, turning his attention for the first time towards George. "What were you doing, boy?"

"I think it's obvious what they were doing," Johnson said. "They were stealing laundry from the Negro neighborhoods."

"The niggers?" Sean exclaimed. "What were you doing in that neighborhood, boy?"

"Uh, well Dad," George began, "you see, it all uh started when we wuz playing baseball. Our neighbors from the other street, well they showed up and..."

"Listen," Sergeant Johnson interrupted, "I don't have time for this and I've already heard this story twice from the boys. Now normally, I'd haul these boys down to the station just like all the other Irish riffraff, but I'll make an exception for you."

"Why me?" Sean asked uncomfortably. He could feel the stares of his friends as they wondered why Sean was being given special treatment.

"Cuz I know your family," the sergeant replied. "You don't live in the slums like these others."

Johnson cocked his head towards the other men in the pub and was greeted by even more hostile looks.

"You and your brothers work hard," the sergeant continued. "Besides, I know that David's grandpa here might get embarrassed if word of this got out. He's a respectable businessman and he don't like to see his name in the papers."

"No, he don't," Sean agreed and then awkwardly added, "thanks."

As Johnson turned his back and headed out the doors, all eyes, especially Sean's, focused on David and George.

"Wait, before you get mad, Uncle Sean," David began, holding up his hands in front of him in a stopping motion. "You need to know that we didn't want to do this."

"Oh really," Sean answered, "and how is it that you managed to do something you didn't want to do?"

"Well, you see, sir," David began, trying to sound as respectful as possible, "it all began, like George said, when these kids from the neighborhood came by our baseball game and picked a fight cuz they said Irish don't belong on the Common. They chased us but we got away and ended up on the hill; then this boy John O'Malley said we should check out the Negro neighborhood. I didn't want to but they all insisted, so we ended up there and before I knew it John wanted to steal the clothes cuz he said they wuz only niggers. I didn't want to but they did anyway, so we had to otherwise they would have never spoke to us again. We worked so hard to make them friends, so we did it and we..."

"Alright, alright, I get the picture," Sean interrupted. "Just be quiet for a minute while I think this whole thing through."

"What's the matter, Sean?" someone shouted from across the pub. "Afraid your kid is just like every other Irish kid?"

"Nah, he's afraid of his boss finding out!" someone else shouted.

Laughter began to fill the pub.

"Now just a minute," Sean interrupted. "I didn't ask that policeman to treat my kids differently."

"I didn't see you stopping him."

"Nah, he seemed to like it."

"He and his brothers have always been treated different since they moved out."

"Yeah, ever since John married that nigger lover."

Sean turned his back to the bar. "Boys, we better go," he said, turning David and George towards the doors.

"Whatsa matter, Sean?" the first man continued. "You too good for us? Gotta leave when it gets a little hot?"

"Of course he does," the man sitting at the table opposite said. "He's always been a coward, afraid to show his face whenever trouble shows up."

"Now you hold on one damn minute," Sean replied, pushing the boys on while he turned to face the man. "I've taken all this grief from you boys cuz I understand how you feel, but I ain't never been a coward."

"You understand how we feel, do ya?" the man answered back, standing up to face Sean. "How would you understand how we feel?"

"Now look, Miles," Sean said, "just because I don't live with you in Fort Hill anymore doesn't mean I don't know what it's like to be Irish. I know how the police treat us and I've felt the same pains you have. I was with you when we left Ireland cuz of the famine; I wuz with you when we arrived and wuz treated like little more than animals; and I wuz with you when we all lived in that little basement at Washington Place. I know what it's like to starve and I know what it's like to be cold, so don't tell me I ain't Irish."

"You may remember those things, Sean," Miles replied, "but you don't feel them anymore. Your blood's thinned living in that nice house and listening to those fancy words. Today just proved it."

"What are you saying, Miles," Sean went on, "that I don't belong here anymore? This ain't your pub to tell me who can and can't come in."

"No, it's our pub," Miles answered, "and we are saying that you don't belong. Now go on you lousy turncoat."

Miles pushed Sean squarely in the chest with both hands. The force knocked Sean back into a table, spilling the beer all over the occupants.

"Why you son of a bitch," Sean yelled as he turned back towards Miles and threw all his weight into a punch to the jaw. The punch hit Miles so hard that a tooth went flying with the blood across the room.

The other two men who had beer spilled on them grabbed Sean from behind and tackled him.

"We gotta help my dad!" George shouted from the entrance. He and David had not yet left the pub, and when the fighting began they turned and ran back inside.

"Dad," George yelled as he jumped on the back of one of the attackers, "don't worry, I'll save you!"

George was still too small to hurt anyone. When the man grabbed him off his back, and threw him, George went flying across the room and into another table. The beer spilled on these men as well, but this time their anger was directed at the man who threw George.

"Did you see what he did to that little kid?" one of them said to the other. "I don't care what Sean has done, you don't treat a kid like that!"

Within moments the bar was in chaos. The few men who were truly angry were joined by others looking for a good fight, and others who were too drunk to know the difference. Tables were smashed, glasses broken, and beer spilled everywhere. Very quickly, George and David realized they needed to get out of the way and the two of them hid under one of the tables still remaining.

"We're in bigggggg trouble," David said to George.

"Uh-huh," George replied as he turned to watch more of the fight.

The next day David, his Uncle Sean, and his Cousin George were all sitting at home watching Sean clean his cuts and bruises. His face had swollen up like a balloon and one eye was swollen completely shut. He had broken one rib and his knuckles had been scraped open when he shattered someone's nose. The fight had lasted only a few minutes but that had been more than enough time for Sean to suffer all kinds of injuries.

"What am I going to do with you boys?" Uncle Sean began, peeling the dead skin off his left hand and throwing it in the trash. "You break the law, steal niggers' clothes, get caught by the police, and then worst of all you get me kicked out of me pub. Just what am I to do?"

Neither boy said a word for fear that whatever they said would be the wrong thing.

"Lord, ever since we moved here, I've felt like a man without a home," Uncle Sean said, more to himself than to the boys. "This ain't my home. The only reason I live here is because William rents it to us, but it's still his and we gotta do what he wants. The only home I ever truly had was back in Ireland. Even when we lived in the slums, when your mother was still alive, George, that was more of a home than this is. This is, I don't know, foreign. It ain't Irish..."

Silence.

"But then," Uncle Sean suddenly went on, "being Irish is what got us into that brawl in the first place."

Uncle Sean paused for another breath.

"Aaahhhh hell, I can't make any sense of it," he finally said, standing up and throwing the bloody towel from his cuts into the trash. "So here's what I am going to do. You boys know what you did was wrong, and I understand that the other boys pressured you into doing it, but that doesn't excuse you. You got to correct what you did and return that laundry."

"All of it?" the two boys whined together.

"No, just the stuff you stole," Uncle Sean answered. "I ain't gonna embarrass you by making you get the clothes back from your friends. I certainly saw today how hard it is to keep friends when you live where we do. You boys worked hard to be a part of that group and despite what you did I still think it's a good group of boys."

"Wow thanks, Uncle Sean," David said in genuine gratitude. He knew that his own father or his Uncle Robert, who also lived with them, would make them get the clothes from the others too. But Uncle Sean had always been cool. Ever since his wife died he'd been kinda more of a friend to George and David, hanging out with them, playing ball, and even shooting darts once in a while. Maybe it was because George was his only son or maybe it was because he didn't like Uncle Robert. Whatever the reason, he was really cool.

"Well, you're welcome," Uncle Sean replied. "I never wanna be embarrassed again by you two, is that understood? Lord knows I may never be able to walk in that pub again. Now you two scat, and make sure that those clothes are returned by tomorrow."

Chapter Five

The Underground Railroad

Lisa woke up again. She couldn't feel her legs or arms and her eyes could see only blackness, so she knew she was still in the box. She rubbed her head gently and felt all the bumps under her hair from the many times she had been thrown around. She could feel them pulsing with her fingers. Some of the bruises were so sensitive that it hurt just to touch them. As she became more alert, she realized she was not on the ship anymore. The smell of the salt in the air was gone, and the box no longer rocked up and down with the waves. She remembered that she had been covered back up and had been taken some distance away from the boat, but that was the last thing she could recall.

Three taps on the top of the box.

"Daddy!" she thought excitedly.

Light suddenly poured into the box and a hand reached in to pull her out.

"Lisa!"

"Daddy!"

Lisa's daddy picked her straight up and held her sitting in his arms. She wrapped her arms around his neck, buried her head in his chest, and the two of them hugged and hugged and hugged. Lisa began to cry.

"Oh, Daddy, I was so scared," Lisa said through sobs.

"Me too, honey, me too," her father replied. He had tears in his eyes as well.

"D-d-daddy," Lisa finally said, pulling back enough to see his face, "are...are...are we free?"

"Almost," her father answered, "almost. We is in Baltimore now."

"Baltimore?" Lisa repeated.

"Yes, Baltimore," he said again. "We still in a slave state, but we is very close to the border now and we got more help here."

Lisa turned her head to where her daddy had glanced and saw a pleasant-looking black lady standing patiently in the corner.

"Lisa, this is Missus Frances Ellen Watkins Harper," he began, "and she is a very important lady to our people. She's free like Mrs. Woodhouse was, but she is also a writer, a poet, and she even travels the country speaking out against slavery."

"Wow," Lisa said, "I never thought that any of the white people would let us do that."

"That's right," Mrs. Harper suddenly said, stepping forward as she spoke, "and I am not the only one. Many of us speak out against this vile slave system. Both blacks and whites have organized anti-slavery groups designed to end this injustice. In fact, you may have heard of a very good friend of mine, Frederick Douglass. He and I write a newspaper called *The Northstar* designed to help bring people, like you, their freedom."

"Wow," Lisa said again, "I would have never dreamed..."

"Dreaming is what it's all about, child," Mrs. Harper went on. "You and your father dreaming of your freedom, our people dreaming of being treated as equals, and all of us, black and white, dreaming of a peaceful world where the color of one's skin makes no difference at all."

"She talks nice, huh Lisa," her daddy spoke up. "Now you can see why she is such an important person and why I know that she can help us."

"Yes, I can help you," Mrs. Harper answered, "like I have helped others. But it will not be easy. Even getting out of

Baltimore is difficult. We will either have to sneak you out or find a way to get you a bond to leave. Then, if you make it to the Northern states you will still have to worry about the slave catchers."

"There's slave catchers in the North?" Lisa asked as she finally got down out of her daddy's arms and stood on the floor. He still had to help her even though her legs had come back to life enough to support her weight. They hurt terribly and as the blood slowly flowed again it brought aching, tingling sensations everywhere as if tiny pins of fire were being pushed into her feet. She shifted back and forth trying to pay attention to Mrs. Harper.

"There certainly are," Mrs. Harper answered, "and there have been even more ever since the Fugitive Slave Laws were passed. A slave catcher can grab any of us, including free blacks like me. We have to prove to a judge that we are free, not the other way around. Even if we have papers, they could be torn up and a slave catcher can claim we are a runaway. You must be very careful because you can trust nobody, not even our own people. Even they have been known to turn in a runaway if there was a big enough reward."

"You mean even if we make it to the free states, we could still be sent back?" Lisa said in despair.

"I'm afraid that's true, young lady," Mrs. Harper answered. "And I'm not sure what we can do about it."

Lisa hung her head in silence. She closed her eyes and began to feel them swell up with tears. Her stomach became queasy and felt like it had dropped down to her feet. Never had she felt this way before. Even when she was working in the hot sun on the plantation or being whipped by the overseer she had never felt as depressed as she did now. She had been looking forward so much towards being free. She had tasted the sweetness of being able to do whatever she wanted and never again having to do what someone else had told her to do. Now, it was being ripped from her. Freedom would not be the sweetness she had imagined. Instead, it would a bitter taste, a tease of freedom, a sense of "you can do what you want, but you'll never be as good as us."

"Hey Lees, cheer up," her daddy said, holding her chin up and wiping away a tear that was forming in her eyes, "we won't have to worry. You just gotta be smart like Mrs. Harper here. As long as we play the white man's game we'll be free. Now you wipe away those tears and let me see a smile."

"Oh yes, yes, young lady," Mrs. Harper added, trying also to cheer up Lisa, "there may be rules we need to follow and problems we have to worry about but you will love being free. There is nothing like it in the world. My goodness I can't imagine what it must be like for you two: Leaving the terrible life of servitude and cruelty to be your own person. What a joy, what a gift! Bless Jesus for he is merciful indeed!"

"Hallelujah, praise Jesus," Lisa's daddy added at the top of his lungs. He looked upwards and continued, "Lord, in all the confusion, I have forgotten to thank ye for all that you have blessed us with."

Then, he broke into a song that he and Lisa had sung at church every week. Lisa added her voice to his and the two of them danced in the joy of the moment. Mrs. Harper clapped her hands and stomped her feet as she too was caught up in their celebrations.

The next evening, Lisa and Jack were treated to the best meal they had ever had in their life. When they finished their meal, Mrs. Harper gave them the instructions they would need to continue their journey.

"Here are two bonds to travel with which I have managed to get from a friend. No colored person is allowed to cross the bridges without them. Unfortunately, this will mean that you cannot take any supplies with you or else the patrols will be suspicious. You will have to live off the land and try to find friendly faces who will help you. One of our codes we use to inform runaways like yourselves is a lighted candle in a window. So far, no one has caught on to this, but you should still be careful that no one is trying to trick you."

Mrs. Harper slid the two pieces of paper across the table. Of course, neither Lisa nor her daddy could read them, but they trusted Mrs. Harper that these were the correct papers.

"Stay away from the main roads and bridges," she continued. "Slave catchers love to patrol these areas."

"But how will we find our way?" Lisa asked in confusion.

"Well, to begin with, my child, you will follow the North Star," Mrs. Harper answered.

"Of course," Lisa said smiling. Even the slaves on the plantation knew the star of freedom that could lead all slaves to the North.

"Then, when you need to get more specific," Mrs. Harper continued, "you will have to be careful and look for road signs. Just remember to try to travel at night and rest during the day. It is the best way to avoid capture."

"Thank you so much for what you have done," Lisa's daddy said, shaking Mrs. Harper's hand, and giving her a hug. "We owe our lives to you and I don't think we'll ever be able to repay you."

"Oh, don't thank me," Mrs. Harper answered, returning the hug to both him and Lisa. "It's the least I could do. And you can repay me by staying safe and free. Now, you had better be going. There's no telling when your luck will run out. Good-bye."

"Good-bye," the two answered back, giving her one last hug. Turning towards the door, Lisa looked up at her daddy with a nervous, excited look on her face. He smiled at her and held her hand saying, "To freedom!"

"To freedom!" Lisa repeated gleefully, stepping out into the city street and heading away.

They ran for weeks. They ran through woods and fields, through streams and rivers, and sometimes over mountains. They rarely used the roads and then only at night. Sometimes the walking was painfully slow because of the darkness. When the moon was full they could see well enough to avoid the sticks and branches. Without moonlight they had to walk with their hands in front of their faces to avoid all the scratches and cuts from the trees, bushes, and thorns. The noises of the owls, crickets, frogs, and flies filled the air. The only time it was truly quiet was in the cool morning air of sunrise.

Lisa had become quite good at recognizing the North Star even when it was partially hidden between clouds. She discovered she could estimate where it was by the position of the other stars. They had only gotten lost twice, they thought, when they kept passing the same rock several times. Lisa thought that they should mark the trees so they could find their way, but her daddy was so nervous about being found that he was against it.

They ate mostly what they could find in the woods. Usually, it was plants and berries, but sometimes Lisa's father would use a large stick to club a squirrel or even a rabbit. Wild animals were not much of a problem except for bears which kept their distance as long as you kept yours. There were no alligators as there had been in Georgia. Occasionally, there were some poisonous snakes. Lisa found herself jumping every time a long dark branch lay half-covered under the bushes.

Several times they had spotted men who could be slave catchers. They had backtracked through streams because they wanted to make absolutely sure that no one could follow them. In a way, it was an exciting adventure to Lisa. Camping out, hiding, hunting, and taking different watches so they did not get surprised. If she hadn't been so afraid of being sent back to slavery (and perhaps to a plantation worse than where she came from, and separated from her father) it might have been fun.

It took them many weeks to travel through Pennsylvania, New York, and into Connecticut. They may have wandered through New Jersey for awhile, but of course they were never too sure of which state they had walked because there were no border markers in the woods. Eventually, they arrived near a town that her daddy felt was a safe place. While Lisa waited anxiously under a bush on the side of the road, her daddy snuck up to a road sign to check their location. He did not know how to read the words on the sign, but Mrs. Harper had written on a piece of paper the names of the important cities and people so that he could match the letters with the sign.

"Yup, it's Farmington," he said as he returned to the woods where Lisa was waiting. "Mrs. Harper said that this was a real good town to stay in. They even have their own anti-slavery society."

"Really?" Lisa asked. She still found it hard to believe that so many white people were against slavery. Well, maybe not so many she thought again. There was that town that Mrs. Harper said to stay away from which prides itself on catching slaves who runaway. They stayed clear of that one for sure.

"Yes," her father answered, "now all we need to do is to find a friendly house and perhaps we will get shelter and a warm meal for a change."

"Oh boy," Lisa said as she broke into a jog, "I can't remember what a warm meal is like. C'mon, Dad!"

"Lisa wait," he shouted through a laugh. "There's no need to run, even if we find a house quickly we can't wake them at this time of night."

It didn't take long for Lisa to find the edge of town. As she walked through the woods looking for a friendly house she made sure not to get too close so as to alert any dogs that might be nearby. After several hours of walking she finally noticed a light up ahead in the distance.

"Daddy, I think I see something," she called to him.

"Sssshhh, not so loud," he said as he came over to the spot where she was crouching. "What did you find?"

"Look," Lisa said, pointing directly in front of her through the large pine tree branches, "there's a light and I think it is a candle on a windowsill!"

"Hhhhmmm, I think it just might be," Daddy said. "Good eyes, love. But remember, we gots to be careful. It could be a trap. You stay here while I go to check it out."

"But Daddy," Lisa protested.

"No buts, girl," he said. "You stay where it's safe while I check it out."

Lisa's father walked slowly towards the house. As he came closer he could tell that there was definitely a candle in the window. He stopped and tried to decide what to do.

He considered waiting 'til morning to see who lived there, but if it was a trick it would be harder to escape in the daylight. He could knock on the front door, but that would be too abrupt and might scare whoever was inside. More than likely they owned a gun and they might shoot first and ask questions later.

He picked up a light rock and threw it against the window to get their attention. The rock made a light bang sound.

He waited: nothing.

He threw another rock.

He waited again: still nothing.

He picked up several small pebbles and threw them all at once. They landed at different times making a noise like a sudden hard rain or hail hitting a rock.

He waited again: still nothing.

He picked up more pebbles this time mixed with dirt. He was about to throw the mixture when a man's face appeared in the window. The man looked out the window but could not see Jack as he was hidden in the dark behind a bush. The man glanced right and left. Then, he took the candle in his hands, opened the window, and held it out towards the woods. He moved it from side to side squinting as he searched for what made the sound, then he brought the candle back in again. He looked out into the darkness again and finally made a waving motion with his hand to show whoever was out there to come inside.

Jack was still unsure but he decided it was now or never. He slowly moved through the woods towards the front door. He remained hidden because he was not sure what to expect. When he was directly in front of the door, he emerged from the woods and slowly approached the door. He knocked lightly three times, then backed away.

The door opened slowly and the man from the window appeared in the doorway.

"Hello?" he said softly.

Jack did not respond. He was standing to the side of the door a little so the man did not see him right away.

"I am a friend," the man said as he slowly stepped a little further through the door. "Don't be afraid."

Jack took a very slow step towards the man.

"Why hello there," the man greeted Jack.

Jack looked at the man nervously but did not answer.

"I am Douglas Washington," he said, holding out his hand, "and I am here to help you."

"Hello," Jack said finally. "Is you a conductor?"

"Why yes I am," the man answered. He turned back towards the door and beckoned to Jack. "Come in, come in."

Jack felt safe enough to follow him. The conductors of the underground railroad were brave people who had dedicated their lives to helping runaway slaves. It was not really a railroad of course, just a very loose organization of people. Most of them did not know one another. They worked alone for the most part, giving signals to the runaways, feeding them, providing them shelter, and sending them on their way. There was no reward for their service and no one knew how many slaves each conductor had helped. How many conductors there were was a mystery, as they had to be so secretive about their work. If their neighbors or the police ever caught them, they could be hanged.

Lisa watched her father walk in the door from her safe spot in the woods. The moon was almost full, and she saw the man smiling and her dad stride into the house. It looked as if she might have a warm meal tonight.

The few minutes that passed while her father was inside seemed like hours, but finally he came outside again and walked into the back yard. He motioned with his hand for Lisa to come toward the house.

"Lisa," he called in a voice little more than a whisper, "come on out. It's safe, honey."

Despite her excitement, Lisa walked slowly and calmly out of the woods. Although there weren't any houses nearby, she felt uncomfortable making any extra noise.

"It's safe, honey, it's safe," her father repeated with a smile on his face. "There's a nice white man and his wife who live here and they would love to let us sleep and eat here."

"Yay!" Lisa said, jumping in the air and waving her arms. "A warm meal, a warm meal. Can we have chicken or ham and greens and tatoes and pie and whatever else we want?"

"Now, now," her father said laughing, "we'll have whatever they give us. Remember that we is their guests and they could get in terrible trouble for helping us. So we'll just take whatever they offer us and be thankful."

"Yeah, I know, daddy," Lisa said with a chuckle. "I'm just so happy!"

"Me too, honey," he answered. "Now let's go inside."

The house was simpler than Lisa expected. For some reason, she had imagined that the house would be well decorated, with riches all about. She did not expect that conductors on the railroad would be poor or have little to share with the slaves they helped. She thought that they would all be rich, highly educated people with time and money on their hands.

These people were nothing like that. Their house had only three rooms. The furniture was simple: a wood table in the center, two beds in the corner room, and a black, wood-burning stove in the center. Their clothes were simple, not much better than Lisa's ("But at least they had shoes," she thought.), and they only had one lantern which they carried around the room with them.

Despite all of this, the two people were wonderful hosts. They gave Lisa and Jack fresh clothes, let them use their bath, put on hot coffee (which Lisa had never had before and didn't really like, but she drank it anyway because it was the first time she had had anything other than water for the past three weeks), and started the stove up so they could cook breakfast.

Lisa felt like a queen. Never before had she been able to take her time in a bath. She washed herself twice to remove all the dirt, dust, and muck from three weeks in the woods. Then she washed herself again just because the water on her skin felt so good. Even though the used clothes that they had given her had to be cut and sewn to fit her, they felt better than anything she had worn before. It was as if a layer of dirty old skin had been peeled off her and replaced by a fresh silky one.

Her father took his time getting bathed and dressed in clean clothes. Mr. Washington even let him borrow his scissors and razor. Lisa laughed as the scruffy beard came off and she could again see her daddy's face the way she had always known it. The whole experience for her became even more enjoyable as the sound of bacon sizzling on the stove and the smell of eggs frying entered into the room.

"Mmmmmmmm, you smell that, Daddy?" Lisa asked.

"Mmmm-hhhhmmm," her daddy mumbled through a half-shaven face. He stopped the shaving for a second and said, "Sure smells good."

"Mmmmmm," Lisa said again, "eggs and bacon. When was the last time we had that?"

"I think it was Christmas," her daddy answered as he stopped shaving again.

"Mmmm-mmm," Lisa said, sticking out her tongue and licking her lips, "I remember that meal. Eggs and bacon and grits and toast. Hey, Daddy, think she'll make grits?"

"Mm-mm," he mumbled.

"You don't think so?" Lisa asked.

"I'm not sure," he answered, washing his face and drying it with a towel. "They eat all kind of strange things up here. But if we gunna be free, we're gonna have to live up here, so we might as well get used to it."

"Breakfast!" a loud voice called.

"C'mon, we better not keep our wonderful hosts waiting," Daddy said as he put the towel down and placed the razor back on the little shelf.

Breakfast was delicious. The eggs were fluffy and fresh (taken from their own chickens this morning, Mrs. Washington had proudly told them), the bacon was not light and not too burnt, and the toast was slightly brown, the way Lisa liked it. The only strange thing was this stuff they called oatmeal. It was kinda like grits, but it was much thicker and drier. When Lisa first put her spoon in it she was able to hold it upside down and the meal just stuck to the spoon without falling.

"Go ahead and try it," Mrs. Washington said laughing. "It will stick real nice to your ribs."

"So," Mr. Washington began when they were almost done eating, "where are you two from?"

Lisa looked nervously at her father. He just looked up from his eggs, fork halfway in his mouth, and said, "No disrespect intended, sir, but I'm not sure if we should tell you. Mrs. Harper warned us not to talk at all about that in case the slave catchers go after us."

"Oh yes, yes, you're quite right," Mr. Washington said. "I plum forgot. That way, even if they come here, they won't know if you stayed here. I'm quite sorry. Well then, can you tell us where you are going?"

"I'm sorry, sir," Jack said again, "but I don't believe I should tell you that either."

"Oh, of course," Mr. Washington said with an embarrassed look on his face, "you're quite right again. But please, if you don't mind. You're the first runaway we've had here for almost a year and every time we meet one of you, we like to hear your stories. It fascinates us to see all the many reasons you run. It may seem obvious that of course every slave would want to escape, but it has appeared to us that it takes a certain kind of person to run and we were hoping that you might help us learn more."

"Well, sir, you are right about that," Jack answered. He felt comfortable talking about his reasons since it would in no way give away where he came from or where he was going, and it was the least he could do in return for the kindness Mr. Washington had shown him. "It does take a special person to run away, but strangely enough I don't think that I am one of those people."

Mr. and Mrs. Washington both looked up from their plates, puzzled by what Jack said.

He continued. "You see, I didn't want to run away for a long time. Now don't get me wrong, I hated slavery like we all hated slavery, but I was not one of those people who runs away. A runaway is different. He or she has a certain courage or determination that I never had."

"Yet, you are here," Mr. Washington said.

"That's right," Jack answered. "But it took a long time to get me here. You see, I never wanted to run when I was a youngster, I never wanted to run when I was working in the fields, I never wanted to run when they whipped me, and never wanted to run even when they sold my wife. Like I said, I hated slavery and wanted to be free, but I had my friends on the plantation, I knew the rules, and I didn't have the courage to go off alone into the unknown and risk death or punishment or being sold again. So, I stayed."

"Well then," Mrs. Washington interrupted. She had completely stopped eating and was listening intently to Jack. "What made you run?"

"She did," Jack answered simply, looking at Lisa.

Lisa turned to face her father. She had never heard this either. Her eyes were focused as she wondered in amazement at what her father was saying.

"It wasn't anything she said or did," Jack explained. "It was just her."

Lisa looked confused.

"You see, on the day she was born my life changed. As I said, I never wanted to run away for me. When it was only me, I just stayed. But then, when she was born, it was no longer just me. Here was this wonderful new life looking up at me with beautiful, innocent eyes. She didn't know hate, she didn't know slavery, she didn't know the difference between black and white. She only knew love. To her, the world was a happy world, a simple world, a world that I knew she would never see again if she stayed on the plantation. I didn't want that. I didn't want her to lose that happiness and feel the horrible depression of endless days of slavery. I wanted her to be free."

Lisa's eyes began to swell with tears. She couldn't believe what her daddy was saying. He'd never said any of it to her. In fact, he never even discussed running away or freedom or anything. He just always seemed interested in getting his work done well and in keeping an eye on her.

"Of course, I couldn't run with her when she was an infant," her father continued. "There was no way she could make the journey. I had to wait until she was old enough to survive on her own. Then, when her mother was sold I had to be even more careful. Every day I thought they was gunna come take Lisa away from me. I knew I had to keep quiet. So I just went about my job. I never messed up and I never complained cuz I figured that it would be easier to run away when the time come if the massah trusted me. I just kept my mouth shut and my eyes on Lisa. I didn't want her to do anything stupid and get sold away before we could run. But she didn't do anything wrong. She was the most precious little girl you ever laid eyes on. She never complained or fussed and she always smiled at me when I came to get her at the end of the day no matter what had happened to her. Y'know it's funny, in a way, spending her childhood on a plantation, slaving in the hot sun, standing knee deep in water day after day harvesting rice, and having to go long periods without rest probably made it easier for her to survive this whole running away thing in the first place."

Lisa's daddy looked around. Everyone had stopped eating, and Lisa had tears in her eyes.

"But now that's all behind us," Lisa's daddy said, breaking the silence. He turned to Lisa with a big smile. "Now we is free!"

$100 Reward

For any information leading to the capture of two runaway slaves.

This summer, two slaves ran away from their plantation near Savannah, Georgia.

One is a girl of roughly 12 years old who answers to the name of Lisa.

The other is her father, Jack, who is reported to be a large Negro with dark bushy hair.

If you have any knowledge of the whereabouts of these two fugitives please contact Mr. F. H. Pettis of New York, agent for the owner.

Chapter Six

Slave Catchers

Harry knocked nervously on the door, and waited.

No response.

He listened at the door. Noises of laughter and loud talking could be heard inside.

He knocked louder.

The noise ceased and a deep voice said, "Charlie, get the door will you?"

"Sure, Mr. Pettis," the voice responded.

Harry heard footsteps. The door opened and inside the entrance was an ugly, dark-haired man smoking a big, brown cigar.

He blew the smoke in Harry's face. "Yeah, whatcha want, kid?"

"My name's Harry Daley," he said through the smoke. "I'm here to see Mr. Pettis about a job."

"Oh yeah," the man replied, "he's expecting you. C'mon in, kid."

Charlie threw the door open wide and allowed Harry to slip in. The room was so smothered in cigar smoke that it was difficult for Harry to see. He moved towards the middle of the room where a long, black table rested. Three men were seated around the sides while a fourth sat at the head of the table, chomping vigorously on his cigar.

"You Mr. Pettis?" Harry said to the man at the head of the table.

"Depends," the man answered. "You Harry Daley?"

"Yes, sir," Harry answered quickly, "I came about the job you posted."

"Yes, so you did, so you did, my boy," Pettis answered. "Well, have a seat here next to Martin."

Harry glanced at Martin who was also chomping on a cigar while rubbing his beard, then he took the seat next to him where Pettis had pointed. Looking around at the other men, Harry realized the kind of people he was dealing with. Each of them had some kind of scar on their face and they all looked at him with malicious eyes and an evil smirk. They could tell Harry was nervous, and these were obviously the kind of men who took advantage of young, naive men like him.

"Welcome to our little group, Harry," Pettis began. "I'm very glad you could join us because today I have some wonderful news to share with all of you. To begin with men, let me introduce you to Harry Daley here. He is a young man from here in New York who has found that he, like yourselves, wants to take advantage of the lucrative business of slave catching."

The other men looked at Harry, still chomping on their cigars, nodding approvingly.

"Harry," Pettis went on, swinging his hand around the table to show off the men seated around him, "let me now introduce you to my employees. On your left is Martin, he is a veteran of the Mexican War and was an excellent scout during his stay there. He has bored of civilian life and wants to use his skills as a scout for a more profitable enterprise."

Martin looked at Harry and smiled through his cigar.

"On the other side of Martin is Bruce. He is a Southerner from Florida who is sick of the heat and wants to spend his summers chasing slaves."

Bruce gave Harry a small smile.

"Directly across from you is Kenneth. He is like yourself, a Northern boy who seeks to make his fortune. Kenneth has shown excellent skill in tracking the runaways and has already found two in the last few months."

Kenneth waved.

"Next to Kenneth is Charlie. He is the one who greeted you at the door, if you remember. Charlie has the best reason to be involved in this business. He used to be an overseer on a plantation in Virginia until one too many runaways forced the master to fire him. I've never seen a man as dedicated and vicious in his work as Charlie here."

Charlie gave Harry a huge grin. The lack of teeth and sinister curve to his lips sent chills up Harry's spine.

"And finally, on the other side of Kenneth is Alex. He too is a veteran of the Mexican War. But when poor Alex returned to his home in Charleston he found that his job had been taken over by a free black who had trained himself as a silversmith and Alex has never forgotten that."

Alex tipped his hat.

"Now that the introductions are over with," Pettis went on, "let's get into the news at hand."

Everyone sat up at attention and Kenneth even took out a paper and pen to take notes.

"As you know," he began, "last month I was contacted by a Mr. Jones from a plantation outside of Savannah, Georgia. He informed me that two of his slaves, a nigger named Jack and his daughter Lisa, had made off sometime in early summer. Charlie and Kenneth have spent much of their time trying to find leads on these slaves' whereabouts, but so far nothing has come up."

He paused, looking around the room, and taking a puff or two of his cigar.

"Until now," he said, smiling. "As you know, I often take out ads in the local papers to try to get information on our runaways. Well, it seems that a first mate on a ship docked in Baltimore saw our ad and contacted an agent of mine. He reports that he spotted the two niggers in the city and headed towards the black side of town. I think he may have known more, but that is all that he will tell us."

"Baltimore," Charlie said, scratching the scar on his left cheek and thinking to himself. "That means they are probably headed up the coast."

"My thoughts exactly," said Pettis. He was glad to see that his men were thinking as well as he was. "That means they are more than likely either here in New York or on their way to Boston."

"Maybe they're in Boston already," Alex said, "or maybe they're on their way to Canada."

"If they're in Canada then we've lost them," Kenneth said.

"They ain't in Canada," Charlie said, taking out a large, black knife with a jeweled leather handle which he then used to clean his fingernails. "I can feel it. They're headed to Boston I tell ya..."

"Oh c'mon," Martin said. "How can you feel where they are?"

"You were a scout, weren't ya?" Charlie shot back.

"Yeah, so?"

"So, didn't you use your feelings to help you find stuff?" Charlie replied, flicking the dirt from his fingernail Martin's way.

"Yeah," Martin said, ignoring the flying specks of dirt.

"So I got a feeling that they are not in Canada; in fact, I bet they're headed to Boston."

"Boston," Kenneth interrupted, "why Boston?"

"I don't know," Charlie said, finally putting the knife down and relaxing everyone. "I just got a feeling. Know what I mean, boss?"

"Yes, I do, Charlie," Pettis answered, "and even though I've gone on your feelings before, I want to play this one a little safer. Jones has already sent me the power of attorney granting me power over these slaves and I want nothing to mess things up. Charlie, you and the new kid, Harry, will follow your feelings and head to Boston."

"Oh great," Harry thought to himself. "Why'd I have to get stuck with that guy?"

"Kenneth," Pettis went on, "you and Martin head to Farmington and see if you can track them down. Farmington is a major stopping point along the road to Boston. And finally, Alex and Bruce, you head to Columbus, Ohio, in case we're way off track. I'll have some of my local boys keep an eye out here in New York. Take these reward posters with you and hang them up wherever you go. Maybe we'll get lucky again. Any questions?"

Harry had a million of them but he was too embarrassed to ask.

"Good, then remember to not damage the property. As you remember, all of my clients are given a guarantee that my men will not damage their property, or else we pay the cost of the slave. And gentlemen, that cost will come out of your hides. Martin, your skills will come in handy up in Farmington. The rains this month have really flooded out the Connecticut River, and if Charlie is right the runaways will need to cross it on their way to Boston. Make sure you patrol the bridges and feel free to hire any local dogs you need. Do any of you need some bribing money?"

"I do," Charlie said, waving his hand. "I wasted it all bribing some nigger lover who didn't know a thing about the slaves we're looking for."

"Hmmpphh," Pettis said, sliding some money across the table to Harry. "You better take this, Harry. Charlie's likely to spend it all in the saloon before you even reach Boston."

Charlie looked menacingly at Harry. It was not a look Harry wanted to see very often.

"O.K., boys," Pettis suddenly said, pushing his chair back and standing up, "let's go get us some runaways!"

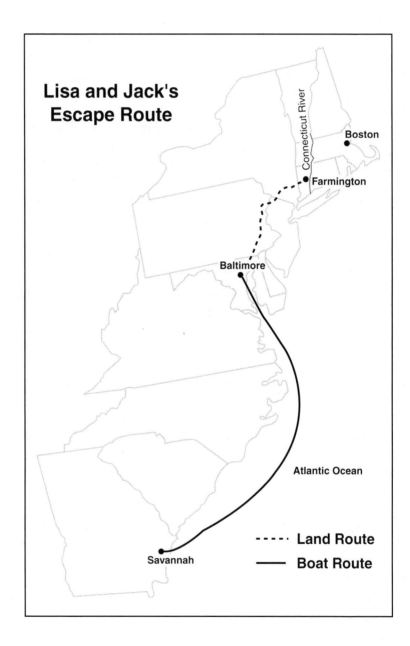

Lisa and Jack's Escape Route

Connecticut River

Boston

Farmington

Baltimore

Atlantic Ocean

Savannah

- - - - Land Route
———— Boat Route

Chapter Seven

The River

"I still can't believe the story you told at breakfast," Lisa said to her father once they were alone.

"Really?" her father said. "Why not?"

"Cuz it's been so long," Lisa answered, "so long since I was born. I can't believe that you and ma been keeping a secret like that for so long. It, it explains so much. Why you worked so hard, why you never complained. I'm afraid to say some of things I thought about you sometimes."

"Well, let's not discuss that now," her daddy said as he piled up some pillows and straw for her. "We still got a long journey ahead of us and we need to get some rest."

"Where are we going, Daddy?" Lisa asked suddenly. "Can't you tell me now?"

"It's funny you should ask that, honey," he replied, "cuz I was about to tell you. We are getting really close now and I think I should tell you just in case something were to happen to me."

"Daddy, don't say that!"

"Well, I need to, honey," he answered. "And you know that if anything were to happen to me, we is close enough that you could make it on your own. Before, you woulda never made it so there wasn't much sense telling you, but now I think I can tell you that we is on our way to Boston."

"Boston," Lisa shouted excitedly, "where all them abolitionists live?"

"That's right, honey," he answered. "The way the white folks back home curse and yell about that city I knew it was a place for us."

"But, Daddy," Lisa said gently, "that's still in the United States where the slave catchers can get us. Why don't we go all the way to Canada?"

"Well, honey, you're not gonna believe this and you're gonna call me crazy, but I'm hoping your mother just might be there."

"Mom? Mom?" Lisa said jumping to her feet. "My mother, she's in Boston? But I thought she was sold, I thought we'd never see her again."

"She was sold," her father said, placing one hand on Lisa's shoulder and settling her down. "But before she left I told her that I was gonna run away with you when you turned 12, and we agreed that she would do the same and that we would meet in Boston if we could."

"But why did you choose Boston back then?" Lisa asked.

"Cuz it was a city we both had heard of. We knew that there would be a way to get there and we figured that once we were there we could always head on to Canada if we felt the need."

"And you think mom's there now?" Lisa asked again.

"Well, she might be," her father answered with a grin. "But don't get your hopes up. Anything coulda happened. She could have been sold further south, or killed; she coulda changed her mind; or she coulda tried and never made it. So let's just wait and see."

"Well, O.K.," Lisa answered slowly. "I'll try, but it ain't gonna be easy."

"I know, dear," Daddy said, "but for now, get some sleep. We gotta get going tomorrow night."

The next evening after they had one more warm meal and another wonderful bath, Lisa and her daddy said their good-byes and thank yous to the Washingtons and were on their way. This time, however, they were able to sneak some food in a pouch. In addition, they were wearing fresh clothes and they even had shoes. Oh how wonderful it would feel to not have your feet being scratched and cut by every thorn bush and stick that happened to be on the ground, Lisa thought with delight.

They walked most of the evening, Lisa again following the North Star, but this time they were walking a little slower than they had before. Although they were both excited to be only one state away from their destination, they were not as worried now that they had experienced a friendly face. By the time it was dawn they had covered very little territory and were even considering going up to the road.

"I'll tell you what," Daddy said to Lisa in a whisper. "I'll go check out the road while you stay here."

"O.K. Daddy but be quick please," Lisa responded.

It took Jack a few minutes to reach the edge of the road and he was still in Lisa's line of sight. She could see him looking up and down the road and even across the way. Then, she noticed him stop and look down. He bent down close to the ground as if he were looking in the dirt; then, he suddenly bolted upright and burst back into the woods.

"Run, Lisa, run!" he yelled as quietly as he could when he got close enough. "Run like you've never run before."

"What is it, Daddy? What is it?" Lisa cried, standing up and turning towards him. Her heart was pounding so fast she felt it would break her ribs.

"Dogs," he called to her. "There's fresh dog tracks in the road and they was with two men, now run!"

Lisa ran faster than she thought she ever could. The trees whipped by her, branches breaking as she past. She moved her feet so fast over the logs and rocks that it was almost as if she were flying. She started to cry as they ran.

"Oh my Lord, oh my Lord," she cried out loud, "they're gonna get us, they're gonna get us."

Her daddy jumped in front of her and grabbed her hand.

"This way," he yelled, turning suddenly to the right.

Fortunately, with the recent rain, the streams seemed to be overflowing with water. They ran in one side and out the other. They ran up and down the stream, then backtracked and exited another side. They gathered branches to cover their tracks. Finally, they rested sitting on a few huge tree limbs, up in the trees.

"Do you think we lost 'em, Daddy?" Lisa asked through panting breaths.

"I think so," he answered, breathing harder than Lisa.

"What makes you so sure they was tracking dogs, Daddy?" Lisa abruptly asked.

"Cuz the tracks weren't straight," he answered. "It was obvious the dogs' feet were moving back and forth as they searched for something. The men's prints were also real close together which means they was walking real slow. If your dog is just going for a walk, he walks fast, and your feet are spread apart. These weren't."

"Couldn't they just be hunters?" Lisa asked hopefully.

"No," he answered. "What would hunters be doing hunting on the road? It's gotta be slave catchers, and even if it ain't we're not taking any more chances. O.K.?"

"Yeah O.K., Daddy," Lisa answered. "So what does that mean we do now."

"First, we'll wait here until nightfall again," he said as he stretched out on the large tree branch. "Then, we'll head south a little away from the road, and then travel due east. Mr. Washington said there's a big river that way, so we gonna have to cross it."

"Ohhhhhhhhhhh, again," Lisa whined, "but we just got new clothes and shoes."

"I know, honey, and I'm sorry, but there's nothing we can do about it," he said softly.

"I know," Lisa said. "I was so enjoying these clothes."

"Me too, me too, honey," her father replied.

The river had not been that far away. When they got there, however, Lisa's heart sank. It was huge, maybe a quarter to a half mile wide, and there seemed to be no safe place to cross.

"It's as big as the Savannah River, Daddy," Lisa cried. "What's it called?"

"That's the Connecticut," he answered in a distant voice that made it obvious to Lisa that he was thinking. His eyes were directed up and down the riverbanks. It was obvious that he was looking for something.

"It's flowing real fast," he commented.

"Think we can cross?" Lisa asked him.

"We gonna have to," he said solemnly. "A big river like this ain't gonna have many bridges and the few it does have will probably be watched. C'mon, take off your shoes."

"Oh, Daddy," Lisa complained.

"Don't worry," he said, "you can tie them around your neck. You're gonna need your feet free to swim."

"We gonna swim here?" she asked nervously.

"Well maybe," he replied. "First, we gonna try to find a log or two we can hold onto. While we look, we'll walk upstream to try to find a better crossing point."

They began walking along the shore. There were lots of different logs lying on the shore as if there had been a flood recently. Unfortunately, the river was getting harder to cross as they walked upstream. White caps were everywhere as the fast-flowing water rushed over the rocks. The noise was so loud that Lisa had to shout to be heard.

"Daddy, I'm scared," she said. "Do we gotta cross here?"

"Here's as good as anyplace else," he answered.

"Can we just wait a while to see if it gets better?"

"It ain't gonna get better. We can stop and rest and eat awhile so you'll be strong enough for the crossing. O.K.?"

"O.K.," Lisa said sitting down.

They sat and ate and watched the river. It seemed almost alive to Lisa now. Like a wide brown snake it moved up and down and back and forth surging water along the shore. It was one of the widest rivers she'd seen and it seemed to be getting wider. One moment it looked one size, then the next moment it would shrug, stretch, and grow some more. As it flowed, it carried with it all kinds of debris from upstream. There were lots of logs, sticks, and branches in the water. Once in awhile she would see something that a human had lost like a broken carriage wheel or a bottle. One time she saw a little toy doll.

"Well, Lisa," her daddy said, standing up and wiping off his pants, "I guess it's time. Take off your shoes."

Removing their shoes and tying them around their necks, Lisa and her father walked into the water while pushing a big log floating along the top.

"At least it's not too cold," Lisa thought as the water began to rise above her waist. She pushed the log forward, wrapping her arms around it as she kicked the water below.

"Listen carefully, Lisa," her father said from his side of the log. "We can steer this thing with our kicks. When we need to turn, one of us will kick harder and the other will drag their feet. You listen for my instructions. O.K.?"

"O.K., Daddy," she responded, "that sounds easy enough."

At first, it was relatively easy. With Lisa and her father kicking hard the log made its way across relatively straight. But then, as they came to the faster flowing water in the middle of the river the log began to spin worrying Lisa.

"Kick, Lisa," her daddy yelled as he dragged his feet.

"Now," he shouted as they began to turn too much, "stop kicking."

"Kick again," he shouted as they again turned too much the other way.

"Stop!"

"No, I'm sorry, kick harder," he yelled. Lisa could hear the panic in his voice.

"Kick, kick!" he yelled again.

"I'm trying, I'm trying," Lisa shouted.

They began to spin as the water moved faster and faster. Within moments they had been caught in a current and the log turned directly into the flow. Lisa was now in front of the log and her daddy was in back.

"Hold on!" he yelled.

Lisa held on as tight as she could. Water was splashing in her face. They had completely lost control of the log.

"Daddy, what do we do?" Lisa screamed over the noise of the rushing water.

"Just hold on!" he yelled, "hold on."

Suddenly, up ahead Lisa saw white caps. That meant lots of rocks.

"Daddy," she screamed, "there's rocks ahead!"

"Try to kick around them!" he yelled.

Lisa kicked desperately to one side. It did no good. She kicked the other way which caused them to speed faster to the rocks.

"Daddy-y-y-y-y-y!" she screamed.

The log smashed straight into a rock. The impact was so sudden that Lisa's father was flung forward into her. Her head banged against the rock and she lost her hold on the log.

"Lisa!" her father screamed as she went under.

He frantically swept his hand through the water looking for her and keeping one hand on the log.

"Got her!" he yelled triumphantly, pulling her back onto the log.

"You alright?" he asked as he placed her securely on the log again. They were safe for the moment as the log had wedged between two rocks.

"I guess so," Lisa answered, rubbing her head and spitting water out of her mouth. "But I lost my shoes."

"I thought I lost you," he said smiling.

"Daddy, look out!" Lisa screamed.

He turned around to see another log coming towards them, but he had no time to turn. The log rammed into Lisa's father, smashing him in the head, and sending him flying into the river.

"Daddy-y-y-!"

"Daddy!"

"Daddy?"

There was no sign of him. Lisa continued to hold on tight to the log. Her body started to shiver and she began to feel very cold.

"Daddy?" she said again.

He was gone.

Chapter Eight

The Meeting

"C'mon, George," David called to his younger cousin, "we'll never get there and back if we don't hurry!"

"I'm coming, I'm coming," George grumbled. "But I still don't see why we have to do this in the first place. They're just a bunch'a niggers."

"Yeah, maybe so," David said. "But they're still people and we still stole from them. At least, your dad said we could do it secretly instead of having to give the stuff back personally."

"Yeah, I guess so," George agreed. "But I still think it's stupid."

"Just hurry up," David pleaded with him.

They made their way to the bottom of Beacon Hill, and began climbing the bumpy, brick streets. The going was slow because they had to keep watch for any police or other person who might report them.

"It's ten times harder returning clothes than stealing them," David thought humorously.

The boys finally made their way to the alley where they found the clothes the first time and slipped in unnoticed. It was almost impossible to see. During the day it had been dark enough, but at night the moon hardly shone through the narrow entryways and David and George had to walk very slowly for fear of stepping into a stairway or pothole.

Within ten minutes, they reached the now empty laundry line and were about to put the clothes back on when George called to David, "Hey, David, look."

"What?" David said, turning around and looking where George was pointing.

"Oh no," David said, "now what do we do?"

There were empty laundry lines everywhere. Apparently, when they had stolen the clothes the first time, the neighbors emptied their lines in fear of losing their clothes as well. Now, it would be impossible to figure out which line they had stolen from.

"Let's just leave them here," George said, dropping the laundry on the ground in front of him and walking away. "My dad didn't say anything about hanging 'em back up, and the owner will find them soon enough."

"Oh well, alright," David said. He was in no mood to argue with George, and it seemed as good an idea as any at the time.

"Hey, George, wait up," David called to him.

It didn't take long for the boys to leave the alley. Once out, they were much more comfortable. Although it was perhaps a little uncommon to see two white boys hanging around the black side of the hill this late in the day, it was not unheard of.

"Thank God that's over with," David said at last.

"That's for sure," added George. "I hate wandering through this neighborhood."

"You do?" David asked, pointing left to indicate that the two of them should turn down the next street. "How come?"

"What do you mean, how come?" George asked David in an annoyed voice. "Don't you feel like you're walking with a target on your back?"

"What do you mean?" David asked innocently.

"C'mon," George said, "don't tell me that you never felt like all the niggers was watching you, as if they was saying, 'Hey, there's another white boy, what are they doing here?'"

"Well, I guess so," David answered slowly. "I just never let it bother me."

"Well, it bothers me," George quickly responded. "It ain't right. Everytime I walk through here, which ain't that often I tell you, I feel like a different person, like I'm guilty of something. It just ain't right."

"Yeah, I guess," David said. "But don't you think they feel that way when they walk through our neighborhood?"

"Yeah, maybe," George answered. "But they're niggers, what do you expect?"

"I guess, well I..."

Suddenly a figure came bursting around the corner and ran right into the two boys knocking them both down.

"What the..."

"Hey!"

"I'm sorry, I'm sorry," the black girl who had bumped into them said, getting up off the boys and looking back to where she came from. "They was afta me and I was just trying to get away. I didn't mean it, I'm sorry."

"Hey, hold on, hold on," David said as he stood slowly and grabbed the girl by the arm before she could run off again. "Who's after you?"

"The slave catchers!" she screamed. "They gonna grab me and sell me back South! Please, let me go! Let me go!"

Instead of letting her go, David grabbed her arm tighter, turning her in the direction where he and George had just come from.

"Hey, David, whatcha doing?" George called to him as he ran to catch up. "Whatcha doing, are you crazy?"

The girl was still trying to push herself free, but David had a firm grip. He made her run so fast she couldn't get any leverage.

"Quick, in here," David whispered as he turned her into the alley where they had just left a few moments ago. "Don't say a word."

George ducked into the alley behind them as the three of them jumped into a little alcove hidden off to the side and ducked down.

"Sssshhhhh," David said to both of them as he put his finger up to his mouth.

"Where'd she go?" a loud voice suddenly called out from around the corner. "She was just here, I could swear it."

"You lose her again?" another voice said approaching. "Damn, I never should have let the boss convince me to let you come along. You're so stupid."

"I'm sorry, Charlie," the first voice answered. "I don't know where she could have gone. She was just in front of me, I swear."

"Yeah, yeah," Charlie said. "Well, don't just stand there letting her get further away, keep moving."

The voices trailed off as the two slave catchers moved on. When they were obviously out of earshot David turned to the girl, and said, "Well, I guess you're safe for now."

"Thank you, sir, thank you," Lisa cried.

"Oh, don't worry about it," David replied matter-of-factly. He had no idea why he had done that. It happened so fast that he really had no time to think. He must be used to hiding from people. "I'm David, what's your name?"

The girl wasn't sure if she should answer. She looked around, looked again at the boys, and finally said, "Lisa."

"Lisa huh?" David said. "Well, Miss Lisa, looks like you owe us big. Why them slavers after you anyway, you a runaway?"

Lisa looked around again thinking for several seconds. Should she trust this boy? What if he was working for the slavers or if he would just turn her in for a reward? Her daddy had said not to trust anybody, but he wasn't here anymore and she needed help. The slavers were bound to come back and she didn't know who to go to in this strange city. Besides, he seemed nice and gentle.

"Promise you won't tell?"

"Yeah, I promise," David answered.

She looked at George, who was staring blankly.

"Oh, yeah, sure I promise too," George said. "Why not, it's not like I'm not in enough trouble already."

"I ran away over two months ago," Lisa began. "My daddy and I left the plantation (she still wasn't going to tell this boy exactly where she came from) and we tried to make it here to freedom. We wuz even hoping that my mom would be here when we got here."

"But where's your daddy?" George asked.

Lisa's eyes filled up with tears. "I don't know," she said. "I think he's dead."

"You think?" George repeated.

"Well, I'm not sure," Lisa went on. "The last time I saw him, we wuz crossing the river when he was hit by a log, went under and I never seen him again."

"Which river?" David asked.

"I dunno," Lisa said, shrugging her shoulders. "Daddy called it the kenny cut or something like that."

"The Connecticut?" George said.

"That sounds right."

"You walked all the way from the Connecticut River to Boston by yourself," George asked as his jaw dropped. "Wow!"

"That ain't that surprising," David interjected. "My mom used to tell me all the stories about the runaways she helped. They ran hundreds of miles through the woods, ate grass, ran from dogs, and did all kinds of things to get here."

"Your mother helps runaways?" Lisa suddenly asked with a hint of hope in her voice.

"She used to," David answered. "But she ain't here anymore."

"Oh," Lisa said quietly as her head fell to her chest.

"But, I can help you," David said quickly and proudly. Suddenly he was excited. He felt important. He *could* help this girl. "I know these alleys alright and I even know a safe place to take you where the slave catchers can't get you."

"You do?" Lisa said excitedly. "You really do? Oh, that would be so wonderful. Thank you kind sir, thank you, thank you."

David felt a little funny being called sir.

"David, what are you doing?" George suddenly said. "You know if we do that, we could get arrested."

"So, we been arrested before, it ain't so bad," David replied with a grin.

"Yeah, but that was different," George said a little angrily. "This is serious. You helpin' a fugitive slave. The police could put us in jail for that."

"They won't put kids in jail," David said. "Besides, we ain't doin' much. All we gotta do is sneak through the alleys to make our way to John Coburn's house. That ain't that far."

"Who's John Coburn?" George asked.

"He's a member of the Boston Vigilance Committee," David answered. "They're the ones who put up those warning signs 'bout the slave catchers."

"Oh," George answered, "where's he live?"

"Right on the corner of Phillips Street, near the top of the hill," David replied. "These alleys should take us most of the way."

"Well alright, David," George answered slowly. "I still don't like it, but you already got us into it. I might as well let you get us out."

"C'mon, Lisa," David said, grabbing her by the hand and raising her to her feet, "we gonna help you stay free!"

The three kids made there way slowly through the alley. It was not as dark as it had been before, David noticed. Perhaps the moon had come out from some clouds, or his eyes had adjusted more. He could see the walls and the turns fairly easily now. He was in the front, leading Lisa by the hand while George was in the back looking nervously to his right and left the whole time.

"How much further?" George whispered.

"Not much," David replied, "but we're gonna have to go on the street now."

They crouched down again, listening to the noises of the street. David poked his head out and looked both ways.

"C'mon!" he said.

They started to run, then quickly slowed down as they realized that running would only attract attention. Everything seemed normal; the few people who were in the streets simply went along with their business, but David and George felt as if everyone was looking at them.

"This place is amazing," Lisa said. "All these colored folk are free: They live in these nice houses, they have their own shops, and their own restaurants, in their own neighborhood. I woulda never dreamed!"

"Yeah, it is pretty neat," George said. "All these niggers, I mean Negroes, living so nice. Almost makes you want to change your skin color."

David and Lisa both looked strangely at George.

"Boy, George," David said, "you really say some stupid things."

"What?" George said in a defensive tone.

"Changing your skin color," David said, "as if you would really want to do that."

"Well no, of course not," George said. "I was just trying to say how nice the nigges, I mean Negroes, live."

"Yeah, whatever," David said. "Maybe you should keep your mouth shut until we get to Mr. Coburn's house."

Mr. Coburn's house was located at the end of the street and was one of the finer looking houses that David had seen in the neighborhood. It was well taken care of and personally attended to. There were no little weeds sticking up anywhere in sight, every brick was in a perfect spot, and even the iron railing on the front steps looked as though it had been recently cleaned.

David looked up and down the street one last time before he lightly rapped on the door.

"Yes, who is it?" a female voice said from inside.

"Please, ma'am, we need help," David pleaded.

The door opened slowly. A pretty black woman placed her face between the small space of the door and the frame. "Yes?" she said.

"Sorry to bother you, ma'am, but we didn't know what else to do," David began. "My name is David and this is my cousin George. We came to you cuz we found this runaway here, and she needs help."

"Oh my goodness," the woman said as she opened the door wide to look at the three children standing on her doorstep. "Come in children, come in."

Lisa and George quickly entered the house followed by David. He took one last look to the left and the right to see if anyone was watching. He thought he saw a man quickly go around the corner, but he wasn't sure.

"Oh, well," he thought as he stepped in to the house. "Must'a been my imagination."

"John! John!" the woman called as she quickly closed the door. "We have some visitors you need to see."

Within moments, a man came into the room, wiping his face with a napkin as he walked.

"Well, well," he said, still chewing whatever he had in his mouth. "What do we have here?"

"Excuse us for interrupting your meal, Mr. Coburn," David said quickly, "but we found this runaway slave running from some slave catchers and we headed to your house cuz my mom had always said that you was one of the smartest, most important Negroes she ever knew."

"Where are these slave catchers now?" Mr. Coburn asked quickly.

"Uh, w-well, I don't know," David replied. "We lost them in the alley, but they could still be around."

"Hhhhhhmmm," he said turning to his wife. "Emmeline, lock the door and keep a sharp eye out for anyone on the street. But first, get these three children something to eat and drink. I am sure they are all hungry. I will take them into the other room to discuss the situation."

"Come along you three," Mr. Coburn said, quickly leading them into the other room where they sat down and waited.

"Well now," he began, "I have seen many strange sights in my day, but I don't think I have ever been disturbed late at night by two young white boys bringing me a fugitive slave. Let's go ahead and start at the beginning. You obviously know me, so why don't you introduce yourselves."

David spoke up for the three of them.

"I'm David, this is my Cousin George, and the girl's name is Lisa. She told me that she ran away from the plantation with her daddy, she got separated from him in the Connecticut River, and she made it the rest of the way on her own."

"My goodness, young lady," Mr. Coburn exclaimed, "you ran all by yourself from the Connecticut River to Boston? That is quite an amazing accomplishment."

"I suppose," Lisa responded. "After I searched the riverbanks for my daddy I did what he told me, and stayed off the roads except to check the signs every once in awhile. I knew that Boston was northeast of the river, so I kept to myself, ate berries, plants, and some other stuff, and here I am. I would have been fine too if I hadn't seen those wonderful breads in the bakery and let the slave catchers see me."

"Fascinating," Mr. Coburn said in reaction to Lisa's story. "And you say you lost your daddy in the river?"

"Yes, sir," Lisa responded with her head hanging low. "He went under after he got hit by a log and I ain't seen him since."

"That's terrible," Mr. Coburn said softly. "But you also said your name is Lisa? What was your daddy's name?"

"Jack," Lisa answered softly.

"Oh my goodness," Mr. Coburn said, sitting back in his large chair. "This is becoming more and more complicated by the second. Young lady, you say your name is Lisa, and you and your daddy ran away from the plantation. Was this plantation by any chance near Savannah, Georgia?"

"Uh-yeah, it was," Lisa replied in a confused tone. "How did you know that?"

"A few days ago," Mr. Coburn began, "a couple of white men came looking through these parts asking a lot of questions. Of course, we keep a watchful eye here especially with our committee, but we have tried to make it a policy to let the men ask their questions so that we can find out what it is they are looking for. It makes it that much easier to outwit them, you see."

He looked around the room at the children, waiting to see if they understood.

"Anyway," he continued, when it was clear that there were no questions, "in my Vigilance Committee meeting the other night, I learned that these two men were looking for a runaway named Jack and his daughter Lisa who had escaped from the plantation in Georgia. We had not yet seen you two, so obviously we could do nothing. Now that you are here, well..."

"Oh no!" Lisa cried, holding her face to her hands. "They found me! They found me!"

"Calm down, calm down," Mrs. Coburn said as she walked into the room with a tray of sandwiches. "We're not gonna let anything happen to you, dear."

She set the tray down on a table and walked over to give Lisa a hug.

"My husband will make sure that you are safe," she said still holding Lisa tight as she cried. "He is a very important man in this city, and we have a well-organized committee that has a lot of experience in dealing with matters like this."

"Yes, that's true, that's true," Mr. Coburn added, handing a sandwich to George and David, and a handkerchief to Lisa. "I have been involved with many instances like this. In fact, I was once arrested after rescuing a fugitive named Shadrach back in 1851."

"But that was different, John," Mrs. Coburn said. "The slave catchers now know that Lisa is here."

"Yes, you're right," he answered, putting his hand on his chin, trying to think of a way to help Lisa. "Our friend here is still so young, we will need someone who can escort her to Canada or at least get her started. She can't stay here, not with the law the way it is and the slavers knowing that she is here."

"Canada," Lisa suddenly said, "I can't go to Canada! I gotta wait here for my daddy, and we gotta see if my mom is here too!"

"Your mother?" Mr. Coburn said in confusion. "How did your mother get into this?"

"Well, I don't know if she is, sir," Lisa answered. "But my daddy said that when I was little, before my mom was sold away, my mommy and daddy agreed to meet in Boston when I turned 12 and I just turned 12 this past May."

"Oh, well this does complicate things even more," Mr. Coburn said. "We've heard nothing about your mother or your father and I certainly won't force you to leave the city until we are sure they are not around. So, I suppose we'll have to hide you."

"Hhhhmmm," he said, thinking to himself. "Where should we hide you? The slave catchers know you are here, so any of our usual hiding places will not be as safe. They will continue to patrol our neighborhood until they find you or think you are gone. So, we need to hide you somewhere else while we somehow convince the catchers that you have moved on. But where should we hide you?"

"She can hide with me," David said suddenly.

George looked at David in amazement.

"Are you crazy, David?" he said.

"No, not at all," David answered. "We got a big enough house and we live far enough away that the slavers won't see her there."

"Well, that's a very nice idea," Mrs. Coburn said, "but we can't..."

"No, wait a minute, Emmeline," Mr. Coburn interrupted. "Maybe this boy has something here. Where do you live, young man?"

"Towards the neck," David answered, "near Dover Street."

"In the south end? That's perfect," Mr. Coburn said. "There's no way the slavers will think to look in that area for a runaway. Do you think you can keep her there for awhile?"

"I don't see that it will be a problem," David replied. "Ever since we left the slums we've all had our own beds, so there is more floor space. I'm sure my Uncle Sean won't mind."

"Wait a minute, wait a minute," George interrupted. "I don't know about this, David. You're getting us in way too deep. Maybe my dad might accept this for a little while, but there ain't no way Uncle Robert would allow a nig, I mean a Negro, to live in our house."

"He will for a little while," David said, "especially if I tell him that Mom has written us and told us Lisa was coming."

"That ain't so," George said. "You haven't heard from your mom in months."

"I know that, but he don't."

"I don't know, David. We could get in a lot of trouble."

"C'mon, George," David pleaded, "stop looking at Lisa for a minute and seeing that she's black. Think about her as a girl. She's lost her daddy, her mommy's been gone for years, and a couple of mean, old slave catchers are trying to take her away and bring her back to being a slave. I know you ain't too fond of these people, but how can we not help her?"

"Well," George said slowly, "I suppose..."

"Great!" David said quickly.

"If we get into trouble this was all your idea."

"Sure, no problem," David said enthusiastically. "Mr. Coburn, what do we do now?"

"Well, son," Coburn answered, "you're gonna have to keep in touch with us on a regular basis so we can alert you to what the slave catchers are doing and if we get any word on Lisa's mommy or daddy. You can't keep coming to our neighborhood because someone might get suspicious. I'll tell you what, there's a man named William C. Nell who lives over at #5 Meeting House on the other side of the hill. He's a friend of Mr. Garrison and a friend to our people. I can get word to him so that he can tell you what is going on. How's that sound?"

"Mr. Nell, #5 Meeting House," David repeated. "I think I can remember that. How long do you think we'll have to hide Lisa?"

"It's difficult to say, son," Mr. Coburn answered. "It all depends on how persistent these slave catchers are and how much they..."

"Bang, bang, bang!" a hand pounded on the front door.

"John! John!" Emmeline called as she ran into the room. "It's the slave catchers. The ones from the other day. They're at the front door!"

"Oh my God!" screamed Lisa.

"Calm down, calm down," John said. "Emmeline, show our three friends to the back entrance and point them into the alleys. I'll answer the door and keep the slave catchers busy."

"Bang, bang, bang," again on the door. "Open up! We can hear you in there."

"Go, go!" John said as he pushed them towards the back of the house.

He opened the door slowly.

"Can I help you, gentlemen?"

"Yeah, you can help us," the older one said. "My boy Harry here says he saw a young runaway and two white kids come to your front door a few minutes ago. She's the one we're looking for and I want to see her now."

"Oh, you must be mistaken," David heard Mr. Coburn saying. Mrs. Coburn had shown them to the back door and they were already heading down the steps into the alley. As the door closed softly behind them, David heard the slave catchers trying to force their way into the house.

"Run!" he whispered.

Chapter Nine

The Doll

"Ssssshhhhh," David whispered, holding his finger to his lips, "everyone's asleep."

David, George, and Lisa managed to make their way home after several twists and turns in the city to throw off anyone who might notice them. But, by the time they arrived at David and George's house, it was already very late and very dark. Opening the back door, the trio walked quietly up the stairs. David opened the door to the second floor apartment and stepped inside.

"This floor is for my family and George's," he whispered to Lisa as he spread his arms over the area in a sweeping motion. It was very dark and Lisa could barely see anything except the moonlight shining through the window on the other side of the room.

"How big is your family?" Lisa asked the two of them.

"Not that big," David answered. "My mom and dad moved to Kansas and are waiting until things quiet down to send for us. They keep saying it will be soon, but it's been over two years now and I'm beginning to doubt it."

"Do you miss them," Lisa whispered, thinking sadly of her father.

"Well yeah, sure I do," David answered. "But most of the time I'm too mad at them to miss them. I mean what kind of parent leaves their kids to go on some crusade to make a state safe for freedom?"

"I don't understand," Lisa said.

"Oh yeah," David realized, "you probably never heard about this, did you?"

"No, I haven't," Lisa answered. "We hear a lot about what's going on in the North, probably more than you think, but I didn't always pay attention. It seemed like it was all another world that I would never see and would never affect me. I was too busy doing my work to really learn about it anyhow. All I remember them talking about Kansas was that a buncha white people killed another buncha white people but that's all."

"Well, it doesn't get much more exciting than that," David said. "It's just a story about people arguing over where slavery can be. No one has decided if it is O.K. for Kansas to have slaves so the government basically said it would be a race. Whichever group got there first and had enough people to make a state would vote whether to have slavery or not. My parents being wonderful abolitionists joined a group of other people from New England. They settled in Lawrence, Kansas, to make sure that there were more free people than slavery supporters."

"But how come they didn't take you?" Lisa asked.

"It's too dangerous," David said smartly, mimicking the way his mother kept reminding him every time he begged to go. "They say it's not safe for their kids and they want us to stay in school. I think they don't want us around cuz lotsa other people brought their kids and nothing has happened to them."

"Who takes care of you?"

"My uncles," he answered. "George's dad, Sean, lives upstairs here with us, and my Uncle Robert lives downstairs with his family."

"Us?" Lisa said, looking around the room. Her eyes had gotten used to the light and she was now able to see several beds with people in them.

"Yeah," David answered, "there's me, my sister Mary who's 10, my brother Thomas who's 9, and my little sister Helen who's only 5."

"And me," George piped in. "I'm 10, but I ain't got no brothers or sisters cuz my mom died when I was little."

"Then, on the other side is my Uncle Robert," David continued. "He and his family got the bottom apartment with the kitchen all to themselves cuz he's older than my dad or my Uncle George. He's got five kids: Joshua, Zachary, Rachel, Ethan, and Jamie. We don't play with them much cuz Uncle Robert makes them go to work like all the other Irish kids. He says school's a waste of time."

"George, is that you?" Uncle Sean suddenly said sleepily from across the room.

"Y-y-yeah, Dad," George replied, pushing Lisa behind him. "We just got back from returning those clothes and we were about to go to bed."

"Everything go alright?"

"Sure, no problem," George answered, "easy as pie."

"Good, now get to bed," he mumbled as he drifted back off to sleep.

"We'd better do what he said," George said quickly.

"Yeah, you're right," David replied as he turned his bed at an angle against the corner. "Here Lisa, I'm gonna sleep on my bed and you lie down in the corner behind me. I'll pile some blankets over you so no one will be able to see you."

Lisa looked at David with blank eyes. She obviously was nervous and unsure of what was going on.

"Don't worry," David said softly, "you can sleep late. Everyone rushes out of here so fast in the morning that no one will see you. My Uncle Sean even leaves for work before sunrise. We'll be home before everyone cuz of school, then we can introduce you. It'll be fine."

Lisa looked at George who was nodding his head in agreement, shrugged her shoulders, and tucked herself into the corner. David covered her with a blanket, got in his own bed, and immediately drifted off to sleep.

Lisa was falling. She was falling fast and water was all around her. She covered her head with her hand so she could see through the water. She was in the middle of a gigantic waterfall and she was falling faster and faster! She looked down to see the bottom but it was so far down all she saw was the vague shapes of the rocks below. She screamed and closed her eyes. She looked again but this time she saw a person standing on the rocks. She focused her eyes harder as she fell closer and closer. It was her daddy! He was standing on the rocks with his arms stretched out to catch her.

"Oh, Daddy," Lisa cried happily. "Oh, Daddy."

He vanished.

Lisa screamed as she fell faster and faster and faster towards the sharp rocks below.

"Dadddyyyyyyyy!" she screamed.

Lisa opened her eyes, gasping for air and sweating. Her eyes moved back and forth. Her breathing slowed down.

"A dream, a dream," she thought. "Oh, it was so scary. Oh, thank God."

She looked around the room trying to remember where she was. She had slept in so many different places in the past three months that it was becoming a big jumble to her. The sun was shining brightly through the window. It was obviously very late in the day. "Had she slept all morning?"

The door opened. Lisa shrank back under her blanket. A girl, dressed in a plain white dress and carrying several books, entered the room followed by a much smaller girl also in a plain white dress. They were obviously sisters with their matching red hair and bright green eyes. The younger one's face was very dirty as if she had been playing in a pile of mud.

"They must be David's sisters," Lisa thought.

"Can we play now, Mary?" Helen asked in her cute little voice. There was a slight whine to it as if she had been asking this question over and over.

"O.K., O.K.," Mary answered. "But I have to get some reading done for school first. Why don't you get your doll out and I'll play with you as soon as I finish."

"But it's no fun playing by yourself," Helen whined.

"Well you're gonna have to," Mary answered.

"Pleeeeeee-ease."

"No, Helen, and if you don't stop asking I won't play with you when I'm done. Now leave me alone."

Mary lay down on a bed about seven feet from Lisa and began to read. Meanwhile, Helen reached under a pillow on her own bed to take out a little toy doll. It wasn't very well dressed, its hair was stringy and dusty, but it was beautiful to Helen just the same.

"Now you listen to me, young lady," Helen made the doll say to an imaginary child, "when I tell you to do something you do it!"

Helen pretended to have her doll slap its child and then go on to some kind of chores. She was obviously playing house with the doll and it must have had a large imaginary family because of all the varied things Helen had the doll doing. It reminded Lisa of her own doll. Without even thinking about what she was doing, Lisa took it out of her skirt and began stroking the doll's head softly.

"You don't have any moving hands or legs like that one," Lisa said to her doll. "But you're just as beautiful."

Lisa's daddy had made her doll from a hardwood stick he had found one day out in the field. He had asked Lisa what kind of doll she wanted and Lisa had told him that she wanted a doll that looked like her mother. He had smiled and patted Lisa on the head and began to work.

It took many weeks to carve the doll. Work on the plantation had not allowed much free time. When Lisa's daddy finally got to work on the doll it was usually late at night. She did not want him to rush it since he was taking great care to make the doll look as much like Lisa's mother as he could. Sometimes she would find him looking at the doll in his hands, then he would turn around to face Lisa with a tear in his eye. Lisa would hug him and say, "I miss mommy too."

When the doll was finally done, Lisa thought it was beautiful. Her daddy had even carved her mother's beautiful long hair flowing down her neck and over her shoulders. It was so beautiful that Lisa kept the doll with her everywhere she went. Even when she worked in the fields she kept the doll in a pocket she had sewn on her skirt and later on a string tied to her wrist. She would sleep with it, eat with it and then when she would play with it she would pretend that the doll was indeed her mommy and have it playing with an imaginary little Lisa.

Lisa stroked the doll more and then slowly began to cry. She couldn't help herself. It wasn't that the doll reminded her of her mommy and daddy. It was everything: not knowing what would happen next, all the running, the slave catchers, the strangers, everything she had been going through for the past two months and longer suddenly overwhelmed her.

Helen stopped playing and looked around.

"Mary," she asked, "do you hear something?"

Mary kept her nose in her books.

"No."

Helen looked around the room. The sound was someone crying. She got up and walked to the corner where Lisa was hiding.

"Mary, there is someone crying and it's coming from the corner behind David's bed."

"Helen, stop playing games, I'm trying to read."

Helen slowly walked to the spot where Lisa was hiding and gently pulled the blanket off. Lisa stared up at her with tears still in her eyes.

"Oh my gosh!" Helen gasped. "Oh my gosh, who are you?"

"I'm, I'm Lisa," the girl said as she tried to wipe her face dry with her arm.

"Why are you crying?" Helen asked.

"I don't know, I couldn't help it," Lisa answered. "I'm sorry."

"What are you doing here?" Helen asked further.

"Uh, ummm," Lisa stuttered, "I'm a friend of David's. He told me to wait here until he got home."

"Are you a friend from school?"

"No."

"Is that your doll?" Helen asked, looking at the item in Lisa's hand that she was still stroking gently.

"Y-yes," Lisa answered. "My daddy made it for me."

"It's pretty."

"Helen, would you stop all the talking," Mary said suddenly as she turned her head towards Helen's direction. "How am I going to get any reading done when... Oh, my God!"

"She's a friend of David's," Helen said as Mary backed up, covering her mouth with both hands. "She seems kinda nice but she's sad and was crying a lot. I told you I heard something."

"Oh, my God," Mary repeated. "Oh, my God. David's gonna be in trouble. Wait till Uncle Robert hears about this!"

"He doesn't need to hear about it," David said panting as he burst into the room. He had run up the stairs as fast as he could when he heard the talking from the apartment. He realized that he was not the first one home.

"Please," he continued, still panting slightly, "please don't tell anyone. She is a runaway slave and she needs our help."

"A runaway slave?" David's little brother Thomas said in an excited voice. He and George had just run into the apartment behind David. "Cool!"

"Why is she here, David?" Mary asked.

"Cuz the slave catchers already know she is in Boston, and Mr. Coburn said that a house like ours was the only safe place in the city to hide her."

"Who's Mr. Coburn?"

"He's this really important colored man," David answered. "He's on all kinds of committees and he's really smart. He even started up that black military company that mom was talking about. Remember?"

"Sort of," Mary replied.

"Well, it doesn't matter. I need you guys to keep this quiet," David concluded. "Otherwise, Lisa could get taken back to the South and she'd never see her mommy or her daddy if he's still alive."

"Can I guard her?" young Thomas asked. "Y'know, to protect her from the bad guys and stuff?"

"She ain't gonna need no guard, stupid," George answered.

"Well, hold on a minute," Mary interrupted. "Maybe Thomas has a point. It's unlikely the slave catchers will find her here. Until Uncle Robert finds out we're gonna have to keep this quiet. Someone will need to make sure that no one comes in here, especially Joshua and Zachary."

"Yeah, they'll tell for sure," Thomas said.

"Can I do something?" Helen asked.

"Sure," David answered, "you can be our little messenger. When we are downstairs during dinner or hanging out, we can send you upstairs to check on Lisa or to bring her food. No one will notice if you leave for a few minutes. Then, I can say you were tired and went to lie down."

"Oh boy," Helen said, "I get to be the messenger!"

"David, this isn't a game," Mary said sternly. "We can get into a lot of trouble."

"Hey, I know that," David answered. "But this is something really important. We can't let Lisa be sent to the South."

"If anyone finds out," Mary warned again.

"No one will find out," David said definitively. "Besides, with mom and dad gone I am the oldest in the family and I make the decisions, so I say she stays."

"Fine," Mary answered angrily, "she stays. But not because you're the oldest. She stays because it's the right thing to do and mom and dad would have done the same."

Chapter Ten

The Family

"Can I be the mother now?" Lisa asked politely.

"But I wanna be the mother still," Helen whined.

"You're always the mother."

"No, I'm not."

"Yes, you are."

"No, I'm not."

"Fine, O.K.," Lisa gave in. "You're the mother. I'm too old to be playing dolls anyway."

"You don't want to play?" Helen said sadly to Lisa.

"No, not really," Lisa answered as she stretched her legs and stood up. "It's getting boring. I'm tired of waiting. When are we going to do something?"

"We are doing something," Helen answered, not understanding what Lisa was referring to.

"No, I mean when are we going to do something about the slave catchers. I've been waiting for over a week now. I am tired of waiting."

"Don't you like playing with me?" Helen's young, high-pitched voice said with a little bit of a shake to it.

"Of course I do," Lisa responded as she sat back down next to Helen and began stroking Helen's fine red hair. "It's just that I am afraid of what is going to happen to me and I want to find out already."

"Don't worry," Helen responded. "My big brother will take care of you. David is the smartest boy in the world. My Uncle Sean says he's smarter than my father ever was."

Lisa smiled at Helen, stroking the younger girl's hair and playing with the dolls again.

The day seemed to drag. Lisa and Helen continued to play dolls while Mary was downstairs preparing dinner for the family. Every day after school the children were supposed to begin their chores. They did most of the housework since they were home before everyone else. With Uncle Robert's five children all working, the only ones who had time to get any work done around the house were George, David, and his siblings. George and David and Thomas usually did the heavy chores such as getting the fire started in the stove and pushing the furniture around to set the dining room up. Mary did most of the cooking with the food that her Aunt Patricia had left out that morning. Sometimes, she had to wait awhile to get started since it was usually David's job to buy the fresh vegetables downtown and he almost always took his time doing it. Helen had to do some light chores, such as straightening out the beds and collecting the laundry. Lisa even did her part by doing most of Helen's chores when the house was empty. She would have done more except that she did not want to go downstairs for fear of being caught. It was because Lisa got so much done that Helen could spend time with her in the afternoon.

"David sure is taking a long time," Lisa said as she looked out the window noticing that it was almost dark.

"Yeah," Helen responded. "Mary said he would be gone awhile because after he went to the market he was going to see that friend of Mr. Coburn."

"I know," Lisa said. "I still would have thought he would be back by now."

As if on cue, the door opened gently as David, George, and Thomas walked into the room.

"Hiya, Lisa," David said as he threw the vegetables on the bed near the girls. "Sorry I was gone so long. I know you've been waiting to hear."

"Oh, it's alright," Lisa responded. "I was starting to worry."

"Don't you ever worry," David answered as he patted her on the leg and sat on the bed next to where he had thrown the vegetables. "We Adamses will make sure you are safe. Right guys?"

"You bet!" shouted Thomas enthusiastically.

"Sure," George added with a lot less enthusiasm. He was still unhappy about the whole thing; however since his dad had said that Lisa could stay, at least until she found out about her parents, George felt it was O.K. to help out.

"Helen, would you bring these down to Mary, please," David said as he handed her the vegetables. "I need to talk to Lisa."

"Ohhhhhh," Helen complained as she stormed out of the room, stomping her feet as she went. "I always have to run the errands up and down the stairs."

David shook his head, rolled his eyes and grinned a little.

"She's always like that," he said.

Lisa returned the smile and waited patiently.

"Well, Lisa," David continued after a pause. He moved closer to Lisa and the bed sagged a little under their combined weight, "I did get a chance to talk to Mr. Nell about the slave catchers. Unfortunately, he didn't have very good news."

Lisa took a deep breath and her heart beat a little faster.

"He says that there is no word on your daddy or your mommy and that more slave catchers have arrived to try to find you. The Vigilance Committee met last night and they have agreed that if your parents don't show up by the end of the week they will have to try to help you move on to Canada."

"I don't want to go to Canada," Lisa shouted in anger as tears began to fill her eyes.

"I know, I know," David said as he tried to comfort her with his hand on her back. "But you may have to. These people know what they're doing and if they think it is best for you to go to Canada then they are probably right."

"But what about my daddy?" Lisa cried.

"I asked Mr. Nell that," David answered. "He said that if your daddy or your mommy show up after you leave they will send them to you."

"Oh, David," Lisa said sobbing, the tears were streaming down her face. "I'm afraid."

"Hey, hey," David said, grabbing some sheets off the bed and giving them to Lisa to wipe her tears. "You don't have to be afraid. There's plenty of people who will take care of you." "I know," Lisa replied, wiping her face with the sheets. "I know they'll take care of me. I feel so alone now."

David didn't know what to say. Lisa was right. She was all alone now. Her daddy was gone. Her mommy might never show. She was all alone in a strange city, hunted by men who wanted to return her to slavery, and hiding out in an Irish house like a cat trying to avoid the dogs. What could David do to help her? What could he say to comfort her?

"I'm sorry, Lisa," he said finally. "I'm sorry. I wish I could say or do more to help you."

"Oh, don't you be sorry," Lisa said quickly, turning her head to face his and taking a big sniff to slow the tears. "Don't you be sorry. You're the one who saved me in the first place. You helped me escape, took me to Mr. Coburn's, and now you've taken such good care of me. You have nothing to be sorry for."

"Yeah, well, I just wish I could do more to help you."

"You've done so much already," Lisa answered. She had almost stopped crying now when she picked up David's hand gently holding it between both of hers. "You really have. You have fed me, talked with me, and helped me pass the time. You've made me feel safe for the first time in months. I don't know what I would have done without you."

David smiled awkwardly at Lisa. She really was a neat girl—not a Negro girl, just a girl. He had never spent so much time with a black person. He now realized as he looked at her that he didn't even think of her as a Negro anymore. He simply thought of her as Lisa.

By the time Mary called them all to help with dinner it was completely dark outside. Lisa, as usual, waited upstairs while everyone else ate downstairs. All the kids were home from work now; the men had also returned and were cleaning up while

Aunt Patricia had arrived in time to help Mary put the finishing touches on dinner.

It was quite an event. Lisa could easily hear all the noise in the kitchen from her corner upstairs. She listened intently as they all talked and laughed with each other. It reminded her of her family back on the plantation—not her immediate family of course, there was only she and her daddy, but her plantation family. There were some people in her family who were related as aunts or uncles or cousins; however, there seemed to be just as many whom she called uncle and cousin who were of no blood relation at all. It didn't matter. On the plantation they were all a family.

After several minutes of random talking and laughing, Lisa heard the chairs being pushed back as the family began dinner. At the head of the table sat Uncle Robert. On his left was Uncle Sean and on his right was Joshua. On the other end Aunt Patricia sat with her daughters Jamie and Rachel on her right and left. The remaining children—Zachary, Ethan, Thomas, George, David, Mary and Helen—filled the spaces in between.

"Joshua, would you say grace this evening?" Uncle Robert said.

"Certainly, father," Joshua replied bowing his head along with everyone else. "Oh, Heavenly Father, we thank you for the food we are about to eat and for the productive day we all had. May you continue to grace this family with your blessings and may you remember those of us who are less fortunate both here in America and in Ireland. Amen."

"Amen," everyone joined in.

Thomas jumped at the food with his fork and the other boys joined in.

"Hey, hey!" Uncle Sean said. "Slow down ye barbarians. There's plenty for us all. No need to act like animals."

"They act like they haven't eaten all day," Aunt Patricia said.

"I haven't eaten since noon and that was almost eight hours ago!" Zachary said as his forked pierced the potatoes.

"Yeah, me too!" Joshua said grabbing the cranberry sauce. It was an impressive meal: potatoes, squash, fresh bread, cranberry sauce, and ham. After they moved out of the slums Aunt Patricia tried to combine foods which she said would honor their new life. In Ireland, life had revolved around the potato. Everyone ate it all the time at every meal. It was so important to their way of life that 12 years ago, when a terrible fungus killed most of the potatoes in Ireland, millions of people died or fled to America. Aunt Patricia always wanted to remember those terrible times by honoring the friends they lost, so every night and at every breakfast some version of a potato was served: fried, mashed, baked, served as a shepherd's pie, in a stew, cut and mixed with peas or carrots or anything else they could find. Tonight, the potatoes were simply mashed.

Their new country of America also had many fine foods that they had never had before. The squash, although not unique to America, was grown locally, and the cranberry sauce was a Massachusetts specialty. Aunt Patricia always wondered whether the children loved it more for its funny red color or the way it made their lips pucker from its tangy flavor.

"How was your work today, Robert?" Aunt Patricia asked.

"The same," he replied. Uncle Robert was never much of a talker.

"And you, Sean," she said, turning to her brother-in-law.

"Hot and stinking as usual," Sean replied as he passed the potatoes down to his son George. "It seems that the summers are only getting longer and hotter every year. I've been working in that factory, what, more than 10 years now, and I still have not found a way to keep cool."

"You gotta hide in the mashing area, Uncle Sean," Zachary spoke up. All three of Uncle Robert's sons worked with Uncle Sean and Uncle Robert at the Felton and Sons Distilleries. Although they were not management as Robert and Sean were, they still got around the company.

"It's nowhere near as hot as the vats," Zachary continued. "And it catches a breeze whenever they make a delivery."

"And how do you know this, young man?" Uncle Robert asked sternly. "I thought you were only supposed to work with the deliveries."

"I do, I do," Zachary answered. "Whenever there's a lull in the work I wander around the company to see what's going on. I'm trying to learn the business like you so I can move up when I get older."

"Hmmmmphh," Uncle Sean said. "That's all well and good, but I wouldn't count on moving up anytime soon in this business. The old man may have let us work there, but he ain't never been a friend of the Irish."

"I know," Joshua interrupted. "We are the only Irish kids there and everyone treats us like we ain't nothing."

"Yeah, they say the niggers are better than us!" Ethan added.

David flinched. It always bothered him the way his cousins made fun of Negroes. He was even more sensitive to it now that Lisa was staying in the house.

"Well, they are," Joshua went on. "They got better jobs than we do and they get a nicer neighborhood than the slums we left."

"Now stop talking this way, boys," Uncle Robert said holding up his hand. "We've had this discussion many times and every time I end it by reminding you that whites are superior to the Negroes. If they have better jobs it's only because the people here in Boston feel sorry for them."

"Yeah, they're kinda like pets," Zachary said laughing.

"More like monkeys," Joshua added with a chuckle.

"Ooohhh, ooohh, oooohh, ooooh," Zachary began as he bent his arms towards his belly and mimicked a monkey.

"Now boys," Aunt Patricia scolded, "I will have none of that talk at the table. I don't care what you think of those people, you will not make those kind of noises at the table. You will not act like animals, at least until you are finished eating."

"Sorry, mom," Zachary said bowing his head.

"Sorry," Joshua added.

"Aunt Patricia," Mary said quickly, trying to change the subject, "will you tell us more of the story."

"Well, I suppose," she answered, "if it will get you all to eat and stop goofing off."

"Yaaaaay," the children shouted.

Aunt Patricia was the storyteller of the family. Storytelling was an old Irish tradition begun long, long ago when there was little to do around the village other than socialize. Indeed, the stories would last hours and sometimes days. Irish men and women would sit around a fire or in a pub and compete to see who could tell the best story. Usually these stories dealt with heroes in the past or with terrible tragedies. (The Irish seemed to love the stories with the sad endings.) But no matter what, the stories always entertained.

At the moment, Aunt Patricia was in the middle of a hero story which she had been telling for two weeks; however, unlike most stories this one focused on events in the recent past and dealt with the tragic death of George's mother, Elizabeth. George had heard his father tell him the story before about how his mother had refused to hide during one of the cholera epidemics in Boston but when Aunt Patricia told it his mother seemed magical. She had told of her birth and her years as a child, always focusing on the good acts that she did in the name of God. By the time Aunt Patricia had gotten to the part where the epidemic struck, George's mother seemed like a saint.

"If you remember," Aunt Patricia began, "when we talked last, the dreadful disease was beginning to hit Boston. It had made its way from Philadelphia to New York and was now attacking us. Most of you won't remember it since it was about 9 or 10 years ago. It was especially terrible in our slums where it spread from home to home like the fire in a forest filled with dry oak. Terror and dismay was in every household. In some instances, where life had departed only a few hours ago, the dead person's corpse would be so swollen that the largest coffin would not contain it; in other cases, the flesh of the dead bodies would fall to pieces, a disgusting mass of death and stench. Amidst this horror, our beloved Elizabeth wandered, trying to comfort the dying and aid the surviving. Sometimes she returned to a residence only a few days later to find that the woman or man had contracted the disease and died within 12 hours. One man, a friend of ours named Chris O'Donnell who lived down the road from us in the old country, died within half a day. By the next morning his body turned immediately black and it became necessary to bury him without delay."

"Disgusting!" Thomas interrupted, sticking out his tongue.

"Eeeeewwww," Helen repeated after him.

"Cut it out," George yelled. "I wanna hear the story."

"Yeah, me too," David added.

"Please go on, Mother," Rachel pleaded.

"Well alright," Aunt Patricia said. "But not until after dinner. All of you stopped eating because you are so interested or so disgusted that you have lost your appetites. I should know better than to storytell at dinner. We will gather around the table after we have cleaned up."

"Ooooohhhh," they all whined.

The rest of dinner was uneventful. Except for a few arguments between Mary and Rachel, the conversation was light and friendly. Once or twice, Thomas managed to hit George in the face with some mashed potatoes but whenever George was ready to hit Thomas back, Aunt Patricia was staring right at him.

When everyone was finished with dinner, David looked up from his plate to see Joshua staring straight at him. He had been doing that for several seconds. Then a sly grin appeared on the side of Joshua's mouth. David knew what he was thinking.

"Can not," Joshua suddenly barked at David.

"Can too," David quickly shot back with a smile.

"Can not!"

"Can too!"

"Can not!"

"Now boys," Aunt Patricia warned. But it was too late. The ritual had started. For several months now David and

Joshua started this game before a wrestling match. It began last year, after David's growth spurt. He was now big enough to give Joshua a fair fight. They began with silly arguments. At the end of a meal they would break into a fight. By now, they had forgotten about the arguments and started right with the bickering before blows were struck.

"Can too!" David yelled as he stood up and faced Joshua.

"Boys," Aunt Patricia said one last time, knowing it would do no good.

"Raaaarrrr!" Joshua yelled as he ran around the table and squared off in the middle of the floor.

"Raaaarrrr!" David joined in.

The two boys began to circle around each other while the rest of the family watched. Uncle Robert and Uncle Sean sat back in their chairs and lit up cigars as they each threw a dollar on the table. They enjoyed these little matches and had even begun placing bets on the winner. So far, Joshua was ahead of David, but Uncle Sean was looking forward to when his own son George could take on Uncle Robert's younger son Zachary.

David grabbed Joshua's left arm with both of his hands. The move caught Joshua off balance and he was swung to the ground. He got up quickly though and tripped David with his left leg but David managed to keep his balance. Joshua then quickly punched him in the abdomen while there was an opening.

"Hey, no kidney punches," Uncle Sean yelled.

Joshua hit David again, this time David managed to block it with his right hand. He countered but Joshua blocked him as well. They each traded a few harmless blows as they circled again and again.

"C'mon!" Thomas yelled.

David wasn't about to disappoint his little brother. Giving a big yell to throw Joshua off guard, David suddenly charged at him, grabbed him at the waist, and tackled him. The two boys wrestled on the floor, both trying to get on top of the other with neither getting any advantage.

"Yuckkkk!" Joshua suddenly screamed, holding his hand up in the air. It was covered with mashed potatoes that Joshua had rolled into during the fight. "Where'd this stuff come from?"

David suddenly stopped and looked around. Joshua did the same. There was a small pile of mashed potatoes in front of Joshua and another pile further away. Joshua looked closer and noticed the trail leading towards the stairs.

"What the heck?" Joshua said in confusion.

"Oh, no," David whispered to himself. He quickly looked around the room in search of Helen realizing she must have taken food upstairs to Lisa.

"Why is there a trail of food going up the stairs?" Joshua asked out loud. His head was bent down following the trail as he slowly made his way out of the room.

"Wait, Josh!" David yelled.

It was too late. Starting slowly and then quickly bounding into a run, Joshua climbed up the stairs with David close behind.

"Wait!" David screamed one last time.

Joshua opened the door of the second floor apartment. In front of him he saw a sight he never imagined to see. Helen was on the floor, playing with her doll and some other toy doll he'd never seen before. Next to her sat a raggedy dressed black girl, fork in hand, ready to take another bite of mashed potatoes.

"Oh, my God!" Joshua cried.

"Josh, Josh," David panted as he reached the top floor.

"You been hiding a nigger up here!" Joshua said turning towards David. "A nigger. Holy crap. Wait till I tell Pa!"

"Wait, Josh, wait!" David pleaded, but it was no use. Joshua had already turned and headed back down the stairs.

"Pa, Pa!" Joshua yelled as he ran. "David's hiding a nigger upstairs. He's hiding a nigger!"

"What?" Uncle Robert shouted as he got up from the table. He looked at his brother Sean who simply shrugged his shoulders and smiled awkwardly. "What are you saying, boy?"

"David's got a nigger," Joshua repeated, still breathing hard from the fight and his running of the stairs. "She's upstairs eating potatoes. I saw her!"

"He's got a nigger?" Uncle Robert shouted angrily. "What the hell does he think he's doing?"

"Robert," Aunt Patricia quietly warned, "hold your temper." Uncle Robert didn't hear her. He was too busy stomping up the stairs with his boys behind him.

"David!" he shouted as his feet pounded up the stairs. "David Adams!"

"Oh, no," David said quietly. His whole body was shaking with fright as he backed into the corner near Lisa. He was in big trouble now.

"I know he's gonna whip me," David thought in fear. "He's gonna whip me good."

"What is going on here?" Uncle Robert yelled as he stormed into the room. "Who are you, girl, and what are you doing in my house?"

Lisa looked at Uncle Robert in terror, unsure what to say.

"She's hiding here, Uncle Robert," David quickly interrupted. He took a deep breath as he stood up straight. He realized that he would have to defend himself. He was beginning to feel a little confident and protective as he tried to be brave for Lisa. "I brought her here last week after I found her running from slave catchers."

"Slave catchers? Last week," Uncle Robert repeated. "You been hiding a runaway here?"

"Y-yes, sir," David answered.

"Over a week this nigger's been in our house," Uncle Robert realized, suddenly turning to his brother Sean who had just walked into the room. "You must'a known, Sean, didn't you."

"Yeah, I did," Sean said defiantly. "The boys brought her to me telling me that she lost her daddy and her mommy and that slavers were after her. I figured the only decent thing to do was to let her stay for awhile 'til that Negro Vigilance Committee gets her outta here."

"And you decided to keep this from me?" Uncle Robert asked angrily.

"Why not?" Uncle Sean replied matter-of-factly. "You ain't the boss."

"I'm the oldest," Uncle Robert shot back.

"So, that don't make you boss over me."

"It sure does," Uncle Robert was shouting right in Sean's face now. "Little brother, you ain't got no right bringing a fugitive in here and risking all of our livelihood without telling us."

"I got every right," Sean shot back. "Besides, you would have sent her out the moment I told you."

"Darn right I would," Uncle Robert answered. "A fugitive's got no place in our house. It's breaking the law and I ain't gonna risk all we've got for no nigger."

"It ain't all yours to risk," Uncle Sean said. "This house ain't even yours. Half of its mine and John's (the other brother in Kansas) and even then we only rent it. So you got no say at all in what I do up here."

"I got every say."

"No, you don't."

"You piece of dirt," Uncle Robert growled as he punched Uncle Sean in the mouth. The punch took Uncle Sean by surprise, but it didn't knock him down.

Uncle Sean punched his brother right back. The fight became violent. Punches were full force and within seconds both men were bleeding.

Uncle Robert backed off panting. He wiped the blood from his lip.

"You son of a bitch," he yelled again as he renewed the fight.

David looked in the corner where Lisa was still sitting and watching in terror. He ran toward Lisa and grabbed her hand.

"C'mon, Lisa," David whispered. "Now's our chance to get outta here."

With all eyes on the fight between the two brothers, Lisa and David easily slipped down the stairs, out of the house and into the darkness of the city.

The Fort Hill Slums

"Report of the Committee of Internal Health on the Asiatic Cholera,
Together with a Report of the City Physician on the Cholera Hospital,"
Boston: J. H. Eastburn, City Printer, 1849.

Chapter Eleven

The Slums

"Where are we going?" Lisa asked, her hand being tugged again and again as David ran down one street and up the next.

"Someplace they'll never find us," David answered mysteriously.

Lisa tripped over a mislaid brick in the road.

"Please slow down," Lisa asked as she regained her balance.

"I'm sorry," David said, stopping abruptly. "I was just scared."

"Well, I was too," Lisa replied. "Don't you think we'll attract attention running through the streets this late at night?"

"Oh, yeah," David said embarrassed. He looked around for the first time realizing how late it was. The streets were extremely dark despite the full moon. The few people on the street were giving them strange looks. David turned quickly and headed in another direction but this time he was walking.

"C'mon," he said. "Fort Hill's this way."

"Fort Hill?" Lisa said, turning and walking on his left and slightly behind him. "Is that a government fort?"

"No, no," David said laughing. "It's the place I used to live, remember? I told you about it the other day."

"Ohhhh," Lisa said as the name rang a bell. "I remember. That was the terrible place where you lived when you were younger. Why are we going there?"

"Cuz not only is it lined with dozens of alleys and hide-outs," David answered with a smart look on his face, "but no slave catcher will ever think to look for you in an Irish slum."

"Oh," Lisa said softly. She wasn't too thrilled with the plan. She had liked David's house. Although she had been sleeping on the floor it was not any less comfortable than all the other places she had slept for the past two months. They had fed her and taken care of her and she had felt welcome there, at least until tonight. Hiding out in some dark, damp slum filled with a group of people who didn't like Negroes was not Lisa's idea of a good time.

David tried to explain to Lisa why his fellow Irish disliked Negroes so much but it still sounded strange to her. He told her how badly the Irish were treated by the people in Boston upon their arrival: How they had trouble finding jobs and decent houses and how they had been forced to live in tightly packed apartments like rats in a cage. They didn't like being the poorest, lowest group in the city. The only ones close to them were the Negroes. David had explained to Lisa what his mother had said about people needing to feel like they are worth something.

"A person," David's mother had said, "needs to feel respected. Many times this means that they need to see themselves as better than someone else. When a person is put down by everyone else around them, sometimes the only way they can feel good about themselves is to find another group to hate and make fun of. That way they feel that there is at least someone else who is worse than they are."

It certainly wasn't right or fair, David had said to Lisa, but there wasn't anything he could do about it. Besides, he had added, not everyone felt that way.

It didn't take long to make it to the wharves. David had felt it was safer to walk along the docks than to cut through the heart of the city. There might be a lot of rude, unruly sailors around but they probably weren't going to bother a couple of kids walking by. Within 20 minutes they were in sight of David's old neighborhood.

"This way," David said, suddenly turning left, "we're gonna head for my friend Frederick's house."

Within minutes of turning left, the fresh smell of the sea was overtaken by the smells of the slum. It was dirty, not a mud and dust dirty, but a fly and crap dirty. An acidic smell of urine and sweat filled the air as well. It was worse at night, David noticed, when the breeze had died down and the thick dank air hung in the streets like a black cloud.

It was noisy. Even though many of the people were asleep, exhausted from a grueling day at work, there were still plenty of sounds coming from the many apartments: a baby crying, a father yelling, a drunk singing, a beggar mumbling, a sick child in pain.

It was ugly. Laundry hung from lines in every direction, from every house. Trash was on the street and in the yards. The two- and three-story apartment buildings had no set order or purpose. They were all slapped together. Sometimes there was a strange space between two apartments and other times there was so little room it looked as if the buildings were fighting each other for space. None of them looked the same. Some were one or two stories high, some were wide, and others were just sheds thrown in front of a building. One might have been an old warehouse, another a reconditioned store and a third someone's old residence. Everything that had once had a different purpose was now a converted apartment.

"People actually live in these conditions? Lisa said in shock. She held her nose and waved her hand in front of her face to get rid of the flies.

"Now you see why we have so much anger and sadness in us," David replied. "It's been like this for years. Families living all in one room, sharing a toilet with five other families or sometimes not even having one, no privacy, most times no beds. It's always noisy and it's always smelly."

"Why don't they move?" Lisa asked in dismay.

"Nowhere to go," David said. "Jobs are never regular enough to save any money."

"But your family has regular jobs."

"That's only cuz my dad married a rich Boston lady, not because of anything we did." David replied in a shameful tone. Even though he loved going to school and living outside of the slums, he was not proud of how they got there.

"You said your daddy had to learn to read to get his job," Lisa returned, still a little confused.

"That's true," David said. "My grandpa said in order for him to get my dad and uncles a job they would have to learn to read. They worked real hard, real fast so I guess in a way they earned their way out."

"Yeah," Lisa agreed. "You did earn it."

"I suppose," David said. "I still feel a little ashamed. Hey, here we are."

He stopped in front of one of the bigger buildings with an outside staircase.

"This is where Frederick lives; he's on the second floor, c'mon."

Lisa followed David up the stairs slowly. A few men in the street too busy drinking to care looked at them curiously.

"We're lucky he doesn't live in the basement," David whispered to Lisa. "Those are the best apartments to live in cuz they are cool; but we would have to go inside, down the dark stairs and flooded floors in order to find anyone. Here we can climb outside to knock on Frederick's window."

Lisa nodded her head to show she was listening. She continued looking around in horror and disgust at the grim surroundings. David stopped in front of a window.

"Stand back down the steps a little so he can't see you," David said to Lisa as he knocked lightly on the glass.

Lisa took three steps backwards. Nothing happened.

David knocked again.

A little boy appeared in the window. He was rubbing his eyes with both fists. David waved and smiled at him. The boy opened the window.

"Who are you?" he asked.

"I'm David Adams," David replied. "I am a friend of Frederick's, is he there?"

"Yeah," the boy said, making no move to get him.

"Well, can I see him?" David asked a little annoyed.

"I suppose," the boy said, giving another stare at David. He stood there another second or two while he thought about what he was doing, then he turned and disappeared for a minute.

David turned, smiled at Lisa, and waved his fist slightly in a triumphant circle.

"He's coming," he said.

The minutes passed like hours. David heard them talking inside and the noise of the drunks down on the street. Someone yelled from the apartment across the street and David jumped.

"David," Frederick said sleepily, as he came to the window, "what are you doing here?"

"Hey, Frederick, how you doing?" David said cheerfully.

"I'm tired," Frederick answered a little annoyed. "What are you doing here?"

"Well, ummmmm," David began. "Uh, I need your help."

Frederick peered out the window to look around.

"Why, you in trouble?"

"Well, sort of," David explained. "I got this friend here who uh, needs a place to stay."

"Where?" Frederick looked around.

"She's on the steps behind me."

"She?" Frederick said a little puzzled.

"Yeah," David said smiling, he knew Frederick would be interested if his friend were a girl. "She's pretty too."

"Well, let me see her," Frederick said anxiously.

"Just a second," David stopped him. "You got to promise to let her stay in your apartment for a couple of nights first."

"My apartment!" Frederick exclaimed. "There's already 12 people living in it already! How am I going to fit another person in here, and where am I going to hide her?"

"Uhhh well," David stuttered, he hadn't thought about that. One thing all these slum apartments never had was space. "Don't you have a spot on the floor so that she could hide under some blankets at night?"

"I guess so," Frederick answered doubtfully. "What about when the sun comes up?"

"Ummmm, well," David thought again, "I could come by before sunrise every morning and to take her out the window and return her in the evening after sunset."

"What will you do during the day?" Frederick said smartly.

"You let me worry about that," David answered quickly. "What do you say?"

"I don't know," Frederick said, squishing his face in thought. "What's in it for me?"

"Ummmmm," David thought again. He didn't have much to offer. He had no money and he had no game or ball or anything else except books to offer.

"I could teach you to read!" David said suddenly.

"Why would I want to read?" Frederick said with a sigh.

"Uhhhhh, well," David thought again. "I could teach you to hit homeruns."

"You would?" Frederick's eyes lit up.

"Yeah, sure. It'd be easy," David answered confidently.

"Well, O.K.," Frederick replied. "Let me see her."

David turned and waved to Lisa to come up the steps.

"A nigger?" Frederick yelled in shock. "You want me to hide a nigger for you?"

"She ain't a nigger, she's a girl in trouble," David said angrily. He hadn't expected this reaction from Frederick. He didn't think Frederick hated Negroes like John O'Malley did. David thought that Frederick did what John did cuz he liked John.

"She's a nigger and I ain't helping her," Frederick said firmly.

"You made a deal," David pleaded.

"That was cuz you tricked me," Frederick explained angrily. "You never told me she was a nigger."

"She ain't a nigger, she's a Negro!" David shouted.

"Whatever," Frederick said as he reached up to the window to close it. "I ain't helping her or you!"

"Wait, please!" David cried, grabbing the window and preventing Frederick from closing it. "She's in trouble. Her daddy has disappeared, her mommy got sold away, and she's all alone in the city with slave catcher's chasing her. You've got to help!"

"I don't got to do nothing," Frederick said angrily as he shut the window on David's hands.

"Aaaarrrrgh," David screamed. Frederick pulled the window back up as David slipped his hands out.

"Now get outta here and don't come back," Frederick yelled, getting ready to slam the window again. "I don't ever wanna see you again, you understand, SOUTHIE?"

The window slammed. Frederick disappeared. David hung his head in despair. He had failed. Lisa had nowhere to go; he had lost his friends. They were all alone.

Chapter Twelve

The Chase

"Now what do we do?" Lisa said desperately.

"I don't know, I don't know," David repeated. "This was the only thing I could think of."

"Should we go back to Mr. Coburn?" Lisa asked.

"Too dangerous."

"What about going back to your house?" Lisa suggested.

"No way," David said firmly. "I'm not going near Uncle Robert till he calms down. He's likely to beat my skin clean off right now."

"Well, we need to do something," Lisa protested.

"But what?"

"Why don't we hide here in one of those alleys?" Lisa said simply. "You said that no one would look for me in this neighborhood. I don't think those people on the street are alert enough to even notice I'm black."

"Hide here?" David questioned with a look of disgust. "On the street in the slums?"

"Sure, why not," Lisa said enthusiastically. "I've slept in worse places. At least we won't have to worry about being eaten by wild animals."

"No, just rats," David said as a chill went up his spine.

"Oh, well anyway," Lisa continued. "It's the only choice we have, unless you have another idea."

"No, I don't," David said, yawning as he slowly began to walk down the stairs. "C'mon, this alley over here is pretty secluded. Nobody will bother us there."

They found a dark spot in the alley that was hidden from the street. For extra protection they even placed some trash in front of them. Then, Lisa curled up in a ball and motioned to David to join her.

"C'mon," she said. "My daddy and I did this in the woods all the time. If you curl up to me with your face near my belly and your knees bent as a pillow for my head it will protect us from the bugs and keep us both warm and comfortable."

David looked at her strangely, shrugged his shoulders, and gave it a try. First, he lay down with his hands under his head. Then, Lisa curled her legs so that he could lay his head on the leg closer to the ground. With his face now staring at her belly, he curled his legs so that she could lay her head on his legs. It actually was quite comfortable. As soon as they got used to the smells and the sounds in the alley they were fast asleep.

"Chuuuuu, chuuuu, heck, heck."

Lisa opened her eyes abruptly. What was that sound?

"Aaaaa-huck, cough cough," the noise continued.

Lisa peered through a hole in the trash to see a large, raggedly dressed man less than 10 feet away holding his gut and throwing up onto the sidewalk.

"David, David," she whispered, moving her leg enough to shake his head. "Wake up. It's morning and someone is throwing up right near us."

"Huh, w-w-what?" David said sleepily.

"Sssssshhhhh," Lisa whispered. "He'll hear you."

"Huh, who?" David was still half-asleep.

"The man losing his dinner on the street over there," Lisa answered gruffly.

"Heck, aaaahhh, eeehhhh, ooohhhh," the man groaned and spit.

"Ohhhh," David said, rubbing his eyes and sitting up. "What a rotten sleep. I feel like I never went to bed. How about you, Lisa?"

"I feel fine," she answered quickly. "I'm pretty used to sleeping anywhere."

"Hmmmm, oh yeah, right," David remembered. "I should have known better."

"Oooohhhhhhh," the sick man groaned one last time. David looked at him as the man collapsed onto the street, passing out.

"Well, don't worry about it," Lisa advised him, ignoring the sick man. "You'll feel fine once you're up and about, with a little food in you."

"Food?" David questioned. "Where did you find food?"

"I...I didn't," Lisa began slowly. "I was hoping you had some idea about that."

"I don't," David said depressed. "It seems I forgot a lot of things when I ran out of the house."

"Well, I guess you'll have to go get some," Lisa said in an "I'm certain that you can do that way," trying to cheer him up.

"Oh yeah, sure," David said awkwardly. "I can uh, get some at the market. My aunt has an account there so I can pick up stuff for dinner sometimes when she's forgotten to give me money."

"Well great!" Lisa said. "You go get the food. I'll wait here."

"Are you sure you'll be alright?"

"Don't worry about me," Lisa assured him. "I could hide all day."

"Well, O.K.," David said, standing up, dusting off his pants and trying to straighten his hair. "I'll be gone awhile. I'm gonna head over to Mr. Nell's house to see if he can give me any advice about what to do."

"Yeah, that sounds like a good idea," Lisa agreed. "You'd better get going while that man is still passed out on the ground."

"Alright," David said, turning his back to her. "Bye."

"Bye," Lisa waved. She turned for another look at the unconscious man in the alley, sat down nervously and waited.

David walked as fast as he could. He didn't want to draw any attention to himself because he wanted to get back to Lisa as soon as possible. He decided to go to the market first since he didn't want to disturb Mr. Nell too early. Then, once he had bought a loaf of bread and some cheese for himself and Lisa he headed to Beacon Hill. As he walked along he couldn't help but notice the peaceful morning air. Birds flew around everywhere, a cool mist was rising from the Common, and the sun was beginning to rise over the buildings. The quiet stillness was calming to David as he slowed his pace and his breathing.

He knocked softly on Mr. Nell's door. The sound of footsteps quickly made their way to the door.

"Hello?" Mr. Nell said opening the door. He was a rather tall man, dressed in a respectable suit. It was obvious that David caught him off guard as his dark hair was still in a mess.

"I'm sorry to disturb you this early, Mr. Nell," David began politely. "We have a serious problem."

"Come in, come in," he said, opening the door wide, leading David in. "I'm sure we'll be able to help you, no matter the problem."

David walked into the house. The door shut quickly behind him. A few moments later a man stepped out of the shadows and into the street.

"That him?" he asked to his partner.

"Yeah, that's the kid alright," Harry said confidently. "That's the one I saw going into the nigger's house with the runaway."

"It's about time," Charlie said, chomping on his cigar while he stepped out into the street. "I knew keeping an eye on that abolitionist's house was a good idea. You stay here and keep an eye out. I'll run to get Kenneth and Martin. I don't want to lose that kid again."

"O.K., Charlie," Harry answered. "Don't forget to bring me some breakfast on your way back, I'm starving."

"Hmmmpphh," Charlie growled as he stomped off.

Sometime later, Charlie returned with some cold sausages, a half-eaten roll, and some bacon.

"Here," he said, handing it to Harry, "it's all I could grab."

"Gee thanks," Harry said sarcastically.

"Anything happen?" Martin asked. He and Kenneth stood right behind Charlie. They had come to Boston several days ago when Mr. Pettis notified them that Charlie and Harry had spotted one of the slaves in Boston. Since then, the men had watched all the abolitionist homes and meeting places hoping for a chance like this one.

"Nothing yet," Harry answered. "I was about to sneak a peak in a window when..."

The door opened. The men quickly jumped into hiding.

"Well, thanks a lot, Mr. Nell," the boy said from the front doorstep. "I'll be talking to you soon."

"Goodbye, young man," Mr. Nell said, closing the door. "And be watchful. The eyes of the wicked are everywhere."

Charlie turned to Harry giving him a big grin.

The door closed. David looked left and right, then he started on his way back to the slums unaware of the slave catchers following him.

By the time David made it back to the slums it was getting close to noon. With the sun directly overhead, the heat had already started to make David sweat. He walked to the hideout in the alley and noticed that the sick man was still passed out on the ground.

"Hey, Lisa, I'm back," he whispered.

"David?" Lisa asked softly.

"Yeah," he answered, handing her the loaf of bread as he stepped around the trash into the hiding spot. "How you been?"

"Fine," she answered. "Not much has happened. The drunk rolled over, moaned, yelled, and went back to sleep. That's about it. What did you find out?"

"Mr. Nell says we'll have to move you," David began. "He says it's too dangerous now and that I've done enough. He gave me the address of a house on the other side of the city. There's people there who can help you get to Canada."

"To Canada?" Lisa repeated, hanging her head down. "I was afraid you'd say that. I don't want to go all alone without my daddy or without you. You've been so wonderful. The first person I felt I could trust since I lost my daddy. Isn't there any other choice?"

"I don't think so, Mr. Nell said that..."

David turned his head.

"You hear that?"

The trash pile suddenly fell forward. Two men stood where it had been.

"Hi, kids," the one on the left said. "Could you tell us which way to Savannah?"

"Run!" David screamed.

David and Lisa ran as fast as they could, but the two men did not give chase. Lisa looked ahead seeing two more men standing in front of them blocking the alley.

"Look out!" she screamed.

David looked behind them. The first two men stood there smiling. He turned his head back. The other two walked slowly into the alley towards them.

"Whatcha gonna do now kiddies?" the first man said from behind them. He smiled wickedly from around the cigar he chomped in his mouth. "There ain't no where to go now."

David looked back and forth again.

"This way!" he yelled, grabbing Lisa's hand as they headed towards the back of the alley.

They ran towards the dead end and stopped. The four men were slowly closing on them with their arms outstretched. David grabbed an old board that was lying against the wall, pushing it to the side.

"In here!" he yelled.

"Hey, where are they going?" the man with the cigar said.

The man rushed up to see a narrow alley so thin that you had to squeeze through sideways to get into it. He called into the alley.

"Come back here you little rats!"

David and Lisa kept squeezing through it slowly. The man tried to follow but the fit was too tight. He backed up.

"Run around the other side you morons!" he called to his buddies.

David reached his hand out of the other side of the alley to grab the wall. He pulled himself out and then grabbed Lisa's hand to help her out too. The slave catchers were rounding the corner.

"Stop you two!" they yelled.

David and Lisa ran again. They took a left down one street and a right down another. As they ran, David racked his brains to try to remember the secret alleys and hideaways in the slums. He used to play in them all the time.

"Stop!" the men yelled again.

The slave catchers were falling behind. David turned a quick corner. A slave catcher stood in front of them.

"They've split up!" Lisa shouted.

David ducked under the slave catcher's grasp leading Lisa to the right. Three of the slavers followed close behind. The street emptied out into a small square. The men got closer. David looked around and headed towards an apartment.

"Where are you going?" Lisa begged. "We'll be trapped there!"

"There's no way out," David yelled back. "Trust me."

David and Lisa bounded up the stairs on the side of the building two by two. A hand grabbed at David's foot but the man stumbled. They reached the landing.

"What now?" Lisa cried.

"Grab this and jump," David yelled as he grabbed one of the laundry lines attached to the top of the staircase. There were only two lines and they each reached to different buildings across the street. David grabbed one line and handed it to Lisa, then he grabbed the other and jumped off the stairs into the air, falling downward to the street below.

Lisa screamed.

David yelled.

"Yahooooooo!"

Near the end of his fall, the laundry line grew taught swinging David through the air away from the house. Lisa smiled and jumped too.

"Yahoooooooo!" she screamed.

Lisa landed on the opposite side of the street at a run. She looked up to see the three slavers at the top of the stairs looking down angrily at them. The men turned and headed down the stairs with a yell.

David's landing was not so smooth. The laundry line was a little too long; David did not have enough time to get his balance before he slammed into the opposite wall.

"David!" Lisa yelled, running towards him. She grabbed him by the shoulders as he shook his head back and forth.

"Are you alright?"

"I think so," he said as he got up slowly. The pain in his left knee was intense and he could already feel it swelling.

"We better move," David said, shaking off the pain. "We've only got a few seconds."

They ran again but this time David had trouble keeping up with Lisa because of his limp. The slave catchers were close behind.

"Head for the waterfront," David called ahead to Lisa.

Heading downhill they started to get a little ahead of the slavers. The momentum made them go faster and faster, and David started to feel like he would make it. Suddenly, his knee gave out and he fell hard on the street. He kept on rolling down the hill until he hit the bottom.

"David," Lisa called to him.

"Run!" David yelled back.

Lisa looked ahead. She looked back at David. One of the slavers caught up to him. David tried to stand.

"Run!" he yelled again at her.

The slaver with the cigar took out a large, black knife with a jeweled leather handle.

"You've been a real pain in the butt, kid," he said as he approached David.

David backed away limping. The man swung his knife striking David's arm. David screamed as the blood began to flow. He stumbled on his bad leg falling to the ground. The man lifted his knife higher.

"You cost me a lot of money in bribes and hotel rent and I'm gonna collect," the man growled at David, lifting his knife even higher.

David closed his eyes, placing his hands in front of his face.

"Noooo!" Lisa screamed, putting her body between the slave catcher and David. "Don't kill him!"

The man's knife stopped in midair.

"Run, David," she screamed. "He won't attack me, he needs me alive to make his money."

David started to run but he couldn't leave Lisa.

"That's right, nigger," the slave catcher said. "But that doesn't mean I can't rough you up a little."

He turned his knife around in his hand and smashed Lisa's head with the butt end. She crumpled to the ground.

"Nooo!" David yelled, running towards Lisa.

Suddenly, David felt a hand on the back of his collar, stopping him in his tracks. He turned around to see a policeman holding him.

"Sergeant Johnson," David cried in relief. "Thank God you've come. You've got to stop these slave catchers from taking Lisa away."

"I'm sorry I can't do that, son," Johnson replied, still holding David firmly by the collar. "They're perfectly within their rights to take this fugitive away. In fact, son, you're under arrest for aiding and abetting a runaway slave."

"What? No, you can't!" David protested.

"Not only can he," the slave catcher interrupted with a huge grin on his face, "by law he has to. Thank you for the help, officer. I'll be seeing you."

The slave catcher picked up Lisa like a rag doll and walked away while Sergeant Johnson dragged David in the other direction.

"No, no, no," David sobbed.

Chapter Thirteen

Hostage

"Alright kid, get outta here," Officer Johnson said as he threw David to the sidewalk.

"Huh, what?" David mumbled as he rolled on the ground.

"I'm not really gonna arrest you," he explained. "That was just a show for the slave catchers."

"I...I don't understand," David said slowly, as he began to get up and dust himself off.

"Listen kid," he began. "I don't like you and I don't like your kind. But I like those slave catchers even less. They come strutting into town with the federal government behind them, thinking they can do whatever they please. They act like they got the Lord's power behind them, strutting into our stations, demanding we help them, causing trouble in our neighborhoods as they stir up the local abolitionists, and just being overall pains in the butts. The law says I got to help them, but no one's got to know I let you go. Besides, if I arrested you, I'd be doing paperwork all night, and my boss would probably yell his head off."

"What about Lisa?" David asked.

"Lisa?"

"The girl I was with," David said desperately. "The one they dragged away."

"The slave?" Johnson replied. "There's nothing I can do for her. She's the property of the catchers now."

"But..."

"No buts," the sergeant interrupted, taking out a hand-kerchief from his back pocket and cleaning David's bloody arm. "There's nothing we can do. Now, you forget about her. Go to school and don't say another word about this."

"But," David complained softly as he rubbed his injured arm. The wound had stopped bleeding now and was starting to burn, but he still could move it.

"Go to school or I will arrest you for truancy!" the sergeant commanded, pointing in the direction of David's school.

David turned and trudged along slowly towards school. What else could he do? The sergeant was right. There was nothing that anyone could do. He should forget about her. But, he couldn't. Lisa was something special. She had treated him like no one else: accepted him for what he was, didn't judge him because of where he lived or because he was Irish. She thanked him for little things that he did, like telling her stories, and she loved him for the big things he had done, like hiding her in his house. She made him laugh and now she was making him cry.

"I gotta do something," he said to himself. "I can't let her become a slave again, I can't."

David continued onto school, his mind racing with ideas. Unfortunately, by the time he reached the school, the only idea he had come up with was some lame excuse as to why he was late. He knew it wouldn't work and that he'd get a beat-ing; however it wouldn't be anything like the one he would eventually get from his Uncle Robert.

"Where ya been?" David's cousin George whispered when David finally took his seat next to him. "The whole family's been worried sick."

"They have?"

"Yeah," George explained. "Uncle Robert really beat the stuffing outta my dad and then ran off to the pub. We haven't seen him or you since. So where ya been?"

"The slave catchers caught Lisa," David said solemnly.

"What? How?" George almost yelled. The teacher turned her head in their direction, so George looked away for a minute.

"How?" he whispered again once she had turned away. "We were hiding out in Fort Hill when they surprised us," David told him. "We ran and ran, but I hurt my leg and fell. Then, this one guy swung a knife at me, and was gunna kill me when Lisa jumped in front of him and saved my life."

"She saved your life?" George wondered in amazement.

"Yeah," David answered. "Then, they knocked her out. I thought we wuz done for but then Sergeant Johnson shows up to help, only he ain't there to help us he's there to help the slave catchers. Then, he holds me by the neck while he watches the slave catchers walk off with Lisa."

"Why'd he help them?" George whispered in confusion.

"He has to remember?" David was losing his patience. He wanted to get out of school and help Lisa. When would it end?

"Oh yeah," George suddenly recalled. "So then, why are you here now?"

"He took me here," David shot back, he could barely stand it now. What was he going to do? "The stupid sergeant took me to school cuz he didn't want to do the paperwork. Now, I'm stuck here and I need to go."

He shouted that last word at George. The teacher turned around looking sternly at David.

"Mr. Adams," she began, "if that beating earlier was not enough, I am sure we could arrange to get you another."

"Sorry, ma'am." David said, bowing his head.

The afternoon lasted forever. David paid no attention to the lesson while he continued to figure out a way to help Lisa. The teacher scolded him several times, but he managed to get the work done enough to keep her off his back. By the time they were finally dismissed, David felt as if his feet would run away without him.

He burst from the schoolhouse and raced towards Beacon Hill.

"David, wait!" George called out but it was already too late. Within seconds David had rounded the corner disappearing out of sight.

"Bang, bang, bang, bang, bang," David's fist pounded on Mr. Nell's front door.

"Mr. Nell, Mr. Nell!" he called. "We've got an emergency! Lisa's been captured, she's..."

David's fist hit thin air as the door suddenly opened.

"Mr. Nell, Mr. Nell!" David shouted again. "Lisa's been taken by the slave catchers, they caught us in our hideout, they..."

"I know, I know," Mr. Nell interrupted, holding up his hand to stop David's panic. "The news spread all over town. Come in my boy and I'll explain."

Mr. Nell led David towards his living room softly shutting the door behind him.

"If you know," David asked as he walked behind Mr. Nell, "how come you're still here?"

"Because, my young friend," he explained as he motioned to David to sit down, "there is nothing we can do at the moment."

"Nothing you can do?" David shouted, standing up again. "I thought...You told me...I mean..."

"Sit down, sit down, son," Mr. Nell said patiently, motioning David again with his hand. "Give me a chance to explain."

David sat down staring quietly at Mr. Nell.

"There is nothing we can do now," he began, "because we have some time. The slave catchers have already spread the word around the town that they have Lisa and will stay in Boston with her for awhile."

"What? But why?" David replied.

"Because, they are hoping to lure her father into town," he answered.

"Lisa's father?" David repeated. "I don't understand."

"The slavers believe that he is still alive," Mr. Nell explained. "They are hoping that he will come to Boston to save his daughter. If he is alive and word gets around he just might try. Furthermore, the slavers get two slaves instead of one resulting in a much more hefty profit. Indeed, I would imagine that he is worth much more than she, perhaps as much as $800."

"Wow," David said under his breath. "Lisa's father still alive."

"Maybe," Mr. Nell reminded him.

"Yeah, but if he is," David thought out loud, "maybe we could somehow trade him for Lisa and then..."

"Hold on, David, hold on," Mr. Nell interrupted. "You've got a sharp mind. I can see that you are already thinking up some bold plan. I suggest you leave that to the Vigilance Committee. They have planned a meeting for tonight. I am sure they will come up with something that will work."

"Tonight?" David said. "Can I come?"

"Certainly not," Mr. Nell answered. "You need to get home before your family worries."

"My family won't care," David said quickly. He had no desire to return home for the beating which was awaiting him. "They really won't. My dad's not living with us anymore, and my Uncle Sean already knows where I am."

David hoped Mr. Nell wouldn't pick up on the obvious lie. He didn't.

"Well," he thought out loud, "you certainly can't come to the meeting; at the same time you've done enough to earn some involvement in this. Why don't you sleep here tonight, I will inform you of our plans when I know more."

David's eyes lit up with excitement.

"Gee thanks, Mr. Nell!"

Later that night David thought he heard a knock on the door. He opened his eyes while he listened from the bed that Mr. Nell set up in his guest room.

"Ssshhhhh," he could hear Mr. Nell whisper. "The boy's asleep in the other room."

"Does he know?" another voice said. It sounded like Mr. Coburn although David was not sure.

"No, he doesn't," Mr. Nell replied. "Are we ready?"

"Ready as we'll ever be," the second voice said. "We need to move quickly before word gets out. The escape route is planned, and we've given him several different kinds of lock picks in case he does get captured. If we go now we should be able to surprise them enough that we may succeed."

"Fine, then let's go," Mr. Nell whispered again as he softly shut the door behind himself.

"Something's going on," David thought to himself. "Something big that they don't want me to know about. But they ain't gonna leave me outta this."

David threw off the bed sheets, put on his shoes, and quickly ran off into the night.

Chapter Fourteen

The Exchange

David followed close behind. There were several men with Mr. Nell, yet he didn't recognize any of them except perhaps for Mr. Coburn. They moved fast, keeping their eyes alert for anyone watching them. David had to be careful not to be seen and once they almost caught him but he managed to duck into the shadows just in time.

"They're heading downtown," David thought to himself.

After a short while the men reached downtown heading towards a hotel. David followed close behind as they walked past the unoccupied front desk and headed up the dark staircase. When they reached the top, they went left towards a door down the hall. David hid at the top of the staircase watching.

Mr. Nell knocked on the door while two men stood behind him and a third one behind them all.

"Who is it?" a voice called out angrily from inside the room.

"My name is William C. Nell and I need to talk with you."

"Go away you abolitionist freak," the voice called again.

"I believe I have some information that will interest you," Mr. Nell called back.

Noises could be heard from inside. The four men waited patiently until the door finally opened.

"Yeah, whatcha want?" said an ugly bearded man with a scar on his face.

"We wish to make you an offer for the slave you have captured," Mr. Nell began, pointing towards the middle of the room where Lisa sat motionless. She was tied to a chair in the middle of the room and her head was slumped forward. When Mr. Nell spoke up, her head began to raise and she looked towards them through black and blue eyes.

"What have you done to her?" Mr. Nell asked suddenly. He was shocked at Lisa's bruised face. Her clothes were all torn, and scratches and cuts covered her arms and upper chest.

"That ain't no concern of yours," the man said with a smile and a laugh. "She's ours to do with as we please. Now, tell me why you're here before I slam the door in your face."

"As I said," Mr. Nell began, trying to turn his attention away from Lisa, "we have come to make you an offer."

"I doubt you have anything that can interest us," the man answered.

"I would not be so sure about that," Mr. Nell said smugly. "Gentlemen, if you please."

The two men behind Mr. Nell separated slightly to show the face of the man behind them.

"Daddy!" Lisa cried, her face lighting up, her body lurching forward as she struggled against the ropes to approach him. "Daddy! Where have you been? What happened? I thought you were dead!"

"The other one!" one of the men inside the room called out suddenly. There was all kinds of commotion in the room as the other slavers came to the door rushing forward to look at Lisa's father.

"How'd you find him?" one of the slavers asked excitedly.

"That will remain our little secret," replied Mr. Nell. "Suffice it to say he survived the Connecticut River crossing and arrived in the city only a short time ago. In fact, we need to thank you gentlemen because if you had not made such a loud noise about your capture of his daughter Lisa, he may never have come out of hiding."

"Get him!" two of them yelled as they ran forward.

"Not so fast, not so fast," Mr. Coburn said suddenly, pulling out a gun from behind Mr. Nell, instantly stopping the slave hunters in their tracks. "This man is ours until we decide otherwise. You want him, you're gonna have to pay."

"With what?" one of the other slavers sneered as he slowly pulled out his own gun.

"With the girl," Mr. Coburn replied, motioning towards Lisa.

"What?" the bearded slaver who opened the door said. "You're crazy."

"Yes, I probably am," Mr. Coburn replied. "But you ain't getting this man without first giving us his daughter."

"What's to stop us from taking both of them," the slaver asked menacingly.

"This gun, for one," Mr. Coburn answered, "and if that don't work, we've already planned an escape for Jack here. By the time you force your way through us, he'll turn tail and run into the streets and you'll never see him again."

"Just shoot the nigger," one of the other slavers said. "I'm sick of this whole thing and I sure as hell ain't gonna let no nigger tell me what to do."

"Hold on, hold on, Charlie," the youngest looking slaver interrupted. "That slave Jack is worth twice as much as his daughter. If we try to take 'em both someone is gonna get killed. Even if it's one of them niggers, the police is bound to stop us and ask us questions. Who knows where that will lead."

"Yeah, Charlie," the bearded slaver at the door added. "Harry's right. You can't go killing niggers whenever you want. Even back home that could get you in trouble."

"Well, gentlemen?" Mr. Nell offered.

"How you gonna do the exchange?" Charlie asked.

"You men will all back away and so will we. Then, you will untie the young lady. She and her father will walk into the middle of the room surrounded by us all. If you make one move towards either of them, we will shoot and both of the slaves will run towards the door. From the middle of the room, Lisa will extend her hand towards us while her father extends his hand to you. Then, once we each have grabbed the hand of the person we desire, we will simply back away and you need never see us again."

"I don't like it," Charlie said.

"Me neither," the man at the door said.

"Yeah, but what do we have to lose?" the fourth slaver said. He had been silent until now partly because he was guarding Lisa. "We got the girl, but you know Mr. Pettis will have our hides if he finds out we let the big one escape. He'll probably take the amount right out of our pay."

"He's right, Charlie," said the bearded man.

"Yeah, I know, but I still don't like it," Charlie said as he began to back up.

"You don't have to like it, you piece of filth, you just have to do it." Mr. Coburn responded, pointing the gun directly at Charlie. He had an intense hatred of the slave hunters and it took all his willpower not to blow them all away right then and there.

"Watch it, nigger," Charlie said with a smile, "or I'll kidnap you and sell you South as well."

"Gentlemen, gentlemen," Mr. Nell interrupted. "There is no need for this idle chatter. We obviously share nothing in common, so there is no need to converse. Simply carry out the terms of the exchange and we can all be on our way."

Both groups of men continued to back up slowly, never taking their eyes off the other for an instant. The man guarding Lisa untied her, threw the rope on the floor, and waved both his hands up in the air.

"There you go," he said.

As the slave hunters continued to back up to the wall, Lisa and her father slowly walked towards the center of the room.

"Daddy," Lisa cried, running forward and opening her arms, "Daddy, I thought you were dead."

"Don't worry, honey," he answered, taking her into his arms and giving her one of his wonderful hugs that she thought she'd never have again. "I'm not dead although I thought I would be in that river. Once I managed to regain some control I headed towards the shore and looked all over for you. When I found your tracks I knew you'd be headed on to Boston so I..."

"That's enough, nigger," Charlie said suspiciously, waving his gun in his hand. "Stick your hand out nice and slow so we can haul you in."

"No, Daddy, don't let go," Lisa cried, hugging him as tight as she could and refusing to let go. "You can't let them take you."

"Don't worry, don't worry," he responded, still hugging her tight. "I'll be fine."

"Sure he'll be fine," the bearded slaver said. "We'll take good care of him. Wouldn't want Mr. Jones' fine property being ruined in any way, now would we boys."

The other slavers laughed.

"It's O.K., Lisa," her daddy suddenly whispered directly into her ear. "I've got lock picks sewn into my shirt and an escape plan all set. You go to safety, you hear?"

"O.K., Daddy, O.K.," Lisa said loudly so they all could hear. She didn't want to ruin whatever plans her daddy and his friends had. "I'll go now."

Lisa stuck out her hand to her left. Her daddy, still staring directly into Lisa's eyes, stuck out his hand in the opposite direction.

"Got you, nigger," the bearded slave hunter said as he grasped Jack's hand.

"Got you," Mr. Nell cried as he grasped Lisa's hand.

"Pow!" a loud shot rang out startling everyone. Mr. Nell ducked as the bullet flew above his head.

"Dammitt!" Charlie yelled.

Before any moves could be made Mr. Coburn reacted. He squeezed the trigger and another bullet flashed across the room hitting Charlie in the stomach.

"Charlie!" the slaver next to him yelled, pulling out his gun and shooting as well.

"Aaarrrghhh," Lisa's father cried as the bullet hit him in the chest.

"Daddy!" Lisa cried.

More shots rang out as everyone with a gun began firing. Lisa frantically ran to her father as Mr. Nell, Mr. Coburn, and his friend backed out of the room.

"Daddy!" Lisa cried, ducking under the rain of bullets, grabbing her father's head, and putting it in her knees. "Oh, Daddy!"

"Lisa," he moaned, reaching up with his right hand to gently caress her face.

"Daddy, don't die, don't die!" Lisa cried. The tears were streaming down her face and mixing with the blood on his chest. "Not after I've found you again."

A large hand grabbed Lisa under the shoulder.

"C'mere you little pain in the butt," the bearded slaver said as he pulled at Lisa.

"Noooo, leave me alone," Lisa cried, still holding on tight to her daddy. "Leave me alone. Daddy, daddy!"

"C'mon, Martin," the youngest slaver said. "Get her and let's get out of here."

David jumped up. The moment that the guns had started firing he knew something had gone wrong. He waited for his chance to see what he could do. When Mr. Nell and his friends backed out of the room, the firing stopped for a second. Everything became suddenly quiet for an instant, then David heard Lisa screaming. He ran in front of the crouching abolitionists and burst into the room.

"Lisa!" David screamed as he saw her being dragged to the back of the room and down the fire escape. A gun fired and David ducked as the bullet took a piece of wood out of the wall next to him.

"David!" Lisa cried amidst her screams and protests. "Help me!"

David swung around. The abolitionists had run back into the room and were kneeling over Lisa's daddy.

"He's dead," Mr. Coburn said.

"Dammitt!" Mr. Nell said, standing up. "We were so close."

"C'mon, c'mon," David said, running towards the back of the room. "We've got to help Lisa."

"We can't," Mr. Coburn said sadly, kneeling over Jack's dead body.

"We can't go running through the streets of Boston in a gunfight," he continued as he shut Jack's eyes and crossed his arms. "Lisa is theirs now and if we try to interfere we will be arrested."

"No," David said simply as he turned to run down the fire escape. He had no time to argue if he wanted to save Lisa.

"They'll head towards the waterfront!" Mr. Nell called to David from behind.

"We can't do anything," Mr. Nell said, turning towards Mr. Coburn. "So we might as well help the kid."

The slave catchers were almost out of sight by the time David had reached the bottom of the fire escape. In the darkness he could barely see them up ahead, however, he could still hear the cries of Lisa whenever she managed to get her mouth away from the bearded slaver's hand. As David followed he continued to pray as he ran, "God, please let me save her, please let me save her."

They reached the waterfront. It was relatively deserted. There were so many boats that David lost track of where they had gone. He looked left. He looked right. They were no where to be seen.

"Help!" Lisa managed to yell out.

David turned to see the slave catchers running onto a ship docked at the other end of the wharf. He ran as fast as he could.

"Lisa!"

By the time David reached the gangplank, the men were all on board. The bearded slaver stood on the ship guarding the entrance with his gun.

"Don't move, kid," he said quickly. "You've caused us way too much trouble and I really would love the excuse to blow you away."

"Please don't take her, please!" David begged.

The bearded man simply smiled as he removed the gangplank from the dock.

"Hey, guys," he called to the other men on board, "let's get this ship moving."

David stood there watching. He didn't know what else to do. Lisa was nowhere to be seen, probably beaten and locked up somewhere. Mr. Coburn and Mr. Nell never showed up. The police certainly would do nothing and, in fact, would probably lock him up if he tried to tell them. Lisa's father was dead, Lisa was being returned to slavery, and David would be all alone again.

The ship began to move away from the dock. David watched it numbly. He couldn't cry, he couldn't run, he just watched. As it began to pull out of sight David was about to say good-bye when his feelings suddenly changed. With a deep breath and a sudden surge of determination David said out loud, "I'll find you, Lisa. Somehow I will find a way to set you free, and I won't rest until I do."

David turned and walked home.

Epilogue

Lisa returned to her master's rice plantation in Georgia where she would work day after day in the hot sun, weeping over her father, and missing her friend David. David would not forget his vow and would shortly leave home to find some way to help his lost friend Lisa. Mr. Nell and Mr. Coburn would return to their work of trying to end the evils of slavery and would always regret the loss of the runaway Jack. They realized that they had no choice in attempting the exchange since Jack was determined to not go anywhere without his daughter. Still, they couldn't help but feel deep regret and sorrow over the loss of Lisa as well.

None of them would have been able to predict the course of events as Civil War grew closer and closer. David would find his plans in chaos, the abolitionists would be frustrated with the slowness of their crusade, and Lisa would spend every day hoping that she would one day see David and freedom again.

Bibliography

Blockson, Charles L. *The Underground Railroad.* New York: Prentice Hall, 1987.

Boyer, Paul S., and others. *The Enduring Vision: A History of the American People.* Lexington, Mass.: D.C. Heath, 1990.

Curry, Leonard P. *The Free Black in Urban America 1800-1850.* Chicago: The University of Chicago Press, 1981.

Engerman Stanley L., and Robert William Fogel. *Time on the Cross, The Economics of American Negro Slavery.* Boston: Little, Brown and Co., 1974.

Escott, Paul D. *Slavery Remembered.* Chapel Hill: The University of North Carolina Press, 1979.

Gibbon, David. *The Old South, A Picture Book to Remember Her By.* New York: Crescent Books, 1979.

Gorrell, Gena K. *North Star to Freedom.* New York: Delacorte Press, 1996.

Handlin, Oscar. *Boston's Immigrants.* New York: Atheneum, 1972.

Hart, Albert Bushnell. *American History Told by Contemporaries.* Vol. 4. New York: The Macmillan Company, 1964.

Horrocks, Thomas. "The Know Nothings." *American History.* Vol. 1, art. 25. Guilford, Conn.: The Dushkin Publishing Group Inc., 1987.

Kent, Deborah. *Boston.* New York: Children's Press, 1998.

Lankevich, George J. *Boston, A Chronological & Documentary History.* Dobbs Ferry, New York: Oceana Publications, Inc., 1974.

Levine, Ellen. *If You Traveled on the Underground Railroad.* New York: Scholastic Inc., 1988.

McCutcheon, Marc. *Everyday Life in the 1800s.* Cincinnati, Ohio: Writer's Digest Books, 1993.

McPherson, James M. *Battle Cry of Freedom.* New York: Oxford University Press, 1988.

Nevins, Allan. "The Needless Conflict." *A Treasury of American Heritage.* New York: Simon & Schuster, (1960), 216-23.

Oates, Stephen B. "God's Angry Man." *American History.* Vol. 1, art. 27. Guilford, Conn.: The Dushkin Publishing Group Inc., 1987.

Quarles, Benjamin. *The Negro in the Making of America.* New York: Collier Press, 1973.

Rae, Noel. *Witnessing America.* New York: Stonesong Press, 1996.

Smith, Julian Floyd. *Slavery and Rice Culture in Low County Georgia, 1750-1860.* Knoxville, Tenn.: The University of Tennessee Press, 1985.

Stampp, Kenneth M. *The Peculiar Institution.* New York: Vintage Books, 1956.

Toledano, Roulhac. *The National Trust Guide to Savannah.* New York: Preservation Press, 1997.

U.S. Government Printing Office. *Black Heritage Trail.* Boston, 1992.

Whitehill, Walter Muir. *Boston, A Topographical History.* Cambridge, Mass.: The Belknap Press of Harvard University, 1963.

Look for this scene in Book Two of the Young Heroes of History Series:
On the Trail of John Brown's Body

"What is it, Pa?" a voice called from the back. Noises could be heard of something being dropped or set down. Then George heard footsteps. Immediately, he became very upset as he realized that David was here, safe and sound, and totally unaware of everything he had put George through.

"Yeah, Pa, what is it?" David repeated as he appeared from behind the counter.

"Uncle Sean!" he shouted as he realized who was standing in front of him. He looked to the right. "George!"

Suddenly, his face was smashed to the side as a fist pounded his cheek. Blood spurted through his teeth and his body was thrown backwards.

"You son of a ——!" George yelled as he let another punch fly. All of the rage and embarrassment he had been holding inside of him was unleashed on David. How could he have left George behind in their grandfather's house when it was his idea to go there in the first place? How dare he take off to Kansas without a word of good-bye? How dare he act as though nothing had happened?